Peeling Back The Layers

S.L. Gandy

©copyright 2024 by Stephanie L Gandy

All rights reserved. This book or any portion thereof may not be reproduced, distributed, or transmitted in any form or by any medium or method without the prior written permission of the copyright owner except for brief quotations for reviews.

www.slgandy.com

Table of Contents

1. That Hospital Gown.......... 9
2. Now... I'm Tired..............29
3. What's With The Blackouts......................35
4. Remember, I'm Professional Rya..............................42
5. Was That For Me..............80
6. The Discussions..............107
7. I'm Not Ok 119
8. Revelations...................140
9. Back To Square One, Huh?................................162
10. All These Emotions.....................181

11. I'm Ready............................206

Scripture Reference Page...............218

Introduction

∞Writing this book has shown me how God can truly take our mistakes, and use them for His glory, and for our good. ∞

Like any book lover, we typically have genres we prefer over others. Personally, I love fiction. I love the creativity that comes along with not only creating an entire world in your mind but also the personality differences that play themselves out in a story. The fact that these stories are completely made up is incredibly fascinating to me. Lately, it seems, there's been an increase in not just dark narratives but demonic characters. I noticed as I continued to read these stories, that my conviction in my faith was stronger. I justified it for quite some time saying that it wasn't that bad. However, there comes a time when we get to our own crossroads as Rya does in the story and The Lord will ask us to choose. As hard as that decision was, I chose and will choose Jesus every time. Funny enough, while deleting all the books that I knew would not meet His approval, I was praying for a solution for my love of books. It wasn't like the desire to dive into a book was gone, just the kind I was reading was being challenged. So, because I love fiction, I figured I would just find other books that were at least Christian, right? Yeah, that search didn't go as well as I expected. Most of the ones I found were just as dark with Christian elements or did not have the narrative I wanted. In seeking The Lord, I heard Him say, 'Write your own.'

    Now, I've written poetry in the past and even short stories, but I never even considered writing a book. If I can be honest, I didn't feel like I could. But Holy Spirit reminded me of all the settings, narratives, and characters I read over the years. The Lord showed me how to write a book that I would love to read but use that to draw people to Christ, and to help people see the Light even in the midst of their trials and tribulations. He showed me that it was possible to be a blessing for people just like me.

Rya is her own character with her own story, but there's so many elements to her personality that relate to my own. Truthfully, each of these characters hold a little piece of my story within theirs. I pray that as you read this book, you find **you** in one or more of these characters and that draws you closer to The One that created us all.

Love and blessings in Jesus Name,

SLGandy

1

That Hospital Gown

Opening my eyes, which are taking longer than usual, I turn slowly to my left, with blurred vision, might I add, wondering where I am. Wait a minute... Something is not right. Why are the lights so bright, and why is my arm hurting? If I'm not mistaken that looks like an IV. Am I in the HOSPITAL?! Why would I be here?! Turning quickly to my right as my vision starts to clear, I come face to face with Jay's shirt, who's leaning over the bed with a frantic expression on his face.

"Ahh!!" I screamed, almost jumping out of my skin.

What in the world is going on? What is Jay doing and why is he leaning over me with this crazed look on his face?!

"Rya, ARE YOU OK!? Thank GOD you're awake. You blacked out!! I tried waking you up before I drove you to the hospital! I didn't know what else to do! One minute you're telling me about the case and the next your eyes are rolling into the back of your head! I had to catch you before you hit the ground! Why are you looking at me like that?! You're not going to pass out again, ARE YOU?!" says John Casey.

AKA, Jay, my personal assistant who is obviously halfway hysterical. Since we grew up in the same neighborhood with our parents as friends, he also thinks he's my little brother. Standing a whooping 6'3, he looks more like my older brother. No wonder I couldn't see anything else. He's standing over me biting his nails as if he needs to tell me something he doesn't want to say. He looks like he's afraid or something. I don't know what's wrong with him.

Still slightly disoriented, I spend the next couple of minutes looking around trying to decipher what he's talking about. Finally with a clearer mindset, I figure it out. I am indeed in the ER, gown and all. They did in fact give me an IV. Wait a minute, if they gave me an IV and I'm in a gown that must mean...I blacked out! Oh no... no no no. I seriously blacked out? I can't believe it happened AGAIN after all these years. No wonder he's so anxious! I know how I would have responded if it was the other way around. He didn't have to take me to the hospital though... Maybe Urgent Care or something. Anywhere but here would have been better. There are so many bad memories here... I already don't like hospitals and to top it off, they put me in a gown like I'm staying. I remember being in this very hospital so many times before when I was younger. Being in this very position with my parents. It's something I thought I'd never deal with again. It brings flashbacks of my parents sitting across from me in this very same ER trying to convince themselves everything was ok, while I sat there in complete turmoil. Not really knowing what was going on with me, made every hospital visit feel like they were going to diagnose me with something terminal. Instead, I didn't receive a diagnosis at all, just occasional blackouts. They couldn't even tie it into heightened levels of stress. Just nothing... Brains fine, nerves are fine. Everything was normal. I still haven't figured out which one is worse because clearly EVERYTHING was not and is not normal. Taking a deep breath so I don't sound as panicked as he looks, I finally take a moment to answer Jay.

"I'm good, Jay. Thanks for looking out for me." I say with a trembling voice.

I smile sadly at him because he looks so worried, so I try to reassure him even through my own frustration and fear. As hard as this is on me, I know it's also hard on him. Ever since we were little, Jay has always looked out for me. Even when he and my little brother were playing cops and robbers, he checked to make sure I was ok. He has seen me have blackouts before, but it's been a long time. Guess that one wasn't the last.

See, I've been having these blackouts since I was a teenager. Even still, the doctors can't find anything solid to help me deal with them. In addition to that, it's been 9 years, 10 months, and 5 days since I've had one, (yes, I'm counting the days). That was right around the time when Lucas... Nope, not going there. Thinking about Lucas won't make this any better. Unfortunately, these blackouts will have to be addressed but I can't focus on that right now. We just got a new case. I wonder if I can convince him to start on the case file since he's still looking at me like I'm going to pass out again. That will give us both something else to focus on.

Instead of easing into asking like a normal person, I just come out with my question. We have a case! Why wait?

"Did you find any information on UFC?"

Looking at me like I've lost my mind, Jay replies,

"Are you KIDDING!? You blacked out right after you gave me the information!"

Well, this is awkward, isn't it? "Oh, right...."

Allow me to explain: Being Rya of RJ Investigation Agency (Rya Jones), I get a lot of calls from the police department to take on cases they don't find that significant or worth the time. For instance, the case I've just been given. This church called Unapologetic Faith Church is the new case. To be honest, I wasn't going to take it initially. I swore off churches a long time ago, but something told me this one was different, so I told Becky to send it over and I'll let her know. I knew she wouldn't have suggested a church if they didn't really need my help. She said they have been getting a great deal pf community calls about break-ins for UFC and practically begged me to take it. Plus, my parents and Jay have been attending for a while, don't ask. Anyways, we just received the information just before my blackout. Can you see my issue now? I finally take the case for a church and then have a blackout which hasn't occurred in almost ten years. You know what, I can't afford to dwell on the past even though I really want to. I'll take my lemons and bury them or whatever that saying is.

Taking a minute to reflect, I can't help but be grateful for the fact that I have work coming in. And with my dad being the former police chief, it gives me a unique perspective on getting this hook-up in the first place. This will also be a good case for Jay to spread his wings, so to speak, since he'll just be graduating with his degree and certification. So, if I can't look on the bright side for me, I'll do it for him. Ok, enough with this rant. I digress.

Back to my original point, Unapologetic Faith Church needs help. The police just think it's some thugs or something, but the church has been persistent in getting to the bottom of these incidents with numerous police reports from different members. You can only imagine how I feel being here in this ER because it's already taking too long for me. It's still my case even if it is a church and since I took it on, I need to get to work. UFC just had a recent break-in, so the information is fresh. I don't want the trail to run cold. Unfortunately, I'm stuck here until the doctors run all the tests for the results of some hidden unforeseen discovery, but they won't find anything. They never do. For Jay's sake, I'll go through the process of getting checked out instead of discharging myself. I just hope they don't take forever. Ugh!!

Looking at Jay, I put on my best sunshine and rainbow voice before I answered. I gotta find a way to draw in my sad demeanor to at least sound convincing.

"Well, no time like the present. I know you have your laptop. We still need answers and to look over that footage, right? How about a compromise. I get checked out while you work. See, win- win."

I give him my brightest smile. He just rolls his eyes, sits down, pulls his laptop out, and logs in while peeking over at me to make sure I don't try to go anywhere.

Jay only had a chance to power up his laptop before I heard a 'knock knock Rya, it's Doctor Chokmah.' I do smile this time because I love Dr. C., I let him know I'm decent and the curtain begins to pull back as Dr. Chokmah, my neurologist walks in. It took me forever to figure out how to pronounce his name. As a teen, I would practice saying Chalk mah before I would go and see him for my neurologist appointments. Unfortunately, that turned out to be a lot, so clearly, I mastered the pronunciation of his name. I told him I wanted to call him Dr. C instead and he smiled and said, 'I like it!' With his laptop already open with my file, Dr. C greets us.

"Well, well! Look who's here to see me. I just so happened to be on call this afternoon when I saw your name on the board. Chart says you had a blackout. It's been years since you've had one if I recall."

"Yep, but I'm good now. Ready to be discharged whenever you are!" I tell him with the same bright smile I just gave Jay.

Dr. Chokmah laughs. "So, what happened?"

He looks down at his laptop to add the notes to my medical summary.

"I have no idea. One minute, I'm talking to Jay. Next thing I know, I'm waking up here in this ER hospital gown."

Yes, I have an attitude. I can't stand these things. I like my goodies wrapped in clothes. I pull my hospital gown a little tighter knowing I don't have on a shirt as my normal distorted form of protection.

"So, who brought you in? JC? Can you tell me what happened?"

Jay stands up and begins to explain. He must really be struggling when he's recalling these events because he's pacing and counting every occurrence on his fingers. Why does he have to pace when he's anxious? He's making me anxious.

"Ok, so about 2:15pm, the call came in from the police department to take the case for the church. We got in the car about 2:17pm to head to the church to meet with Pastor John for the first statement. Pastor Mark joined the meeting a couple of minutes later and let us know that he would be our direct contact for the case. The meeting lasted for 30 minutes which means we left for the office at 2:47pm. We arrived at the office at 3:15pm. Once we arrived, unlocked the doors, and set down our things to discuss the meeting, I noticed Rya's speech started slurring a little. That was about 3:18pm. I asked her was she ok while moving closer to her. She looked at me as her eyes started rolling back into her head and began falling. I immediately caught her before she was able to hit the floor. I called her name repeatedly trying to see if she would wake up. She was breathing but wasn't responding. Carrying her to the car, I put her in and ran back into the office to grab our things. That was around 3:21pm. We arrived here at 3:45pm. While on the way, I kept checking to make sure she was still alive. I held her wrist to check her pulse and kept calling her name. Her pulse was good, but she wouldn't wake up."

Focused, Dr. Chokmah responds with "Huh uh, ok. Thanks JC."

Looking back over at me he asks, "You don't remember feeling different at all this time? No slight headaches or lightheadedness before you got to the office or at the meeting? Have you been under any stress lately, anything unusual, or any recent changes? I know you're getting closer to 40 which might result in some hormonal changes. Have you been feeling any different lately? Any fatigue, lightheadedness, infrequent headaches, changes in your monthly?"

Horrified by the question of my upcoming hormonal changes, I answer out of annoyance and a little embarrassment because who wants to talk about that?!

"No… what does that have to do with anything?"

Being the patient doctor he is, he says, "Your hormonal changes might explain why you had this blackout now when you haven't had one in years. Not saying your hormones or any of these things are the reason but it could give us a basis to start with. Redirecting our focus on these changes may potentially show us what to look for."

"No changes that I can think of, I'm good." I answered confidently.

Dr. Chokmah does his examination while asking me if I'm experiencing any pain, dizziness, lightheadedness or unusual sensation while checking my eyes, ears, throat, head, and limbs. He also does a tilt table test to make sure that sudden movements haven't contributed to the blackout. This is when the doctor makes you lay down on your back with your head off the edge of the table resting in your doctor's hands. Once you're situated, the doctor then takes your head and tilts it to the left and right to check for dizziness, lightheadedness, and sometimes nausea.

Being satisfied that I experienced none of these, he picked up his laptop, and added his last notes.

"OK, good! Well, we'll do the MRI and the blood work just in case. If we don't find anything, you're free to go, sounds good?" Dr C says with a smile on his face.

"Yep! Sounds great to me, doc."

Before leaving to help his next patient, he smiles and says, "Always good to see you Rya and JC. I'll put this paperwork through so they can get you in as soon as they have a tech and a room available."

"Thank you." I said, finally relieved.

I love my doctor. We've been riding since I was 16. I remember having my first blackout and crying profusely because I didn't understand what was going on. He did my examination, set up my MRI referral with the nurse and then sat down next to me while my parents and I waited for the nurse to bring the script. Looking at me and my parents who were seated in the chairs across from us, I knew Dr. C saw the hopelessness on all our faces. He told me that he didn't know what was going on with me yet but, as my doctor, would work hard to find out. He said to us that I could have a normal life even if I had blackouts. I stood on that because at the time my parents didn't know what to say or do for that matter. My mom, being a psychiatrist, felt like she should be able to get some answers, but she couldn't figure it out either. That drove her crazy for a while, but she learned to cope, just like we all did. Dr. C was honest with us but encouraging. He's like a second dad now. Dr. Chokmah is the best Neurologist around if you ask me, even if he makes me get useless MRI's. Because it's Dr. C, I'll be out of here in no time. Like I said, win-win.

After 2 hours of testing and discharge papers, I just realized I hadn't seen my shirt so we can finally go. Jay must have seen the confusion on my face because as I was looking around for it to get dressed, he handed me another one.

"They had to cut off your shirt to get the heart monitors on you. I know you have spare clothes in the car, so I grabbed this one from the trunk while they wheeled you in. Sorry. I know you liked that shirt."

Trying not to pout, I thanked him and got dressed once he left the room. I loved that shirt...

Finally, out of the hospital, Jay wants to take me home instead of the office because he's scared, I'll have another one. Not! Happening!

"Ry, I just think you should get some rest. I don't want you to overdo it and black out again. I mean, I don't want to have to take you to the hospital again if something happens. Maybe I can just call your parents next time, but I don't want to worry them. Although I did call your mom and she's definitely worried! I just think you should go home and reset. The case isn't going anywhere. We can start fresh first thing in the morning. I'll even go to the office to work on it and send you the information

I find. Don't you think that's a good idea?" Jay says with a hopeful tone.

He starts tapping his fingertips on the steering wheel, trying to keep himself calm while he drives. Of course, I volunteered to drive, but oh no! I could black out at the steering wheel. Ugh! I'm telling you he's like the little brother I didn't ask for. Even though his tone tells me he is pleading with me to go home, this is too important to put off.

"Jay, you already know what these blackouts are, and we've already been over this. This isn't anything you haven't seen before, remember? I'm good. I have a clean bill of health from Dr. C. We're going to the office to make some headway with the case. This is not up for discussion. We stayed in that hospital for hours to come out with no answers. I can't let these blackouts dictate my life, Jay. I haven't even had one in years! This could be a one-time occurrence for all we know. I'll sit down, but there's no way I'm not going to the office to work this thing the first chance I get. We might be able to find a lead quickly, but we won't know until we start investigating. Plus, if you try to take me home, I'll just drive myself back without you. You drove today so my car is in the driveway where I parked it, just so you know."

Using that bright smile again for emphasis, he sighs and finally concedes. We live only a few blocks away from each other and he knows my car. He'll be able to see me drive off as I honk my horn driving past and waving with that same bright smile on my face.

"Alright FINE! But will you at least take it easy? I mean for real. I know you. You get started and you forget everything else. How are you feeling though? Was this blackout any different from the ones you used to have? I don't remember your speech slurring like that. Do you feel any different? Were you being honest when you answered the doctor's questions? I mean, you will be 40 in a couple years. Just saying."

"Jay, I love you like a brother, but I will throw this ripped up shirt at you if you don't stop with all the questions! No, I don't feel any different. From what I remember, my speech always slurred right before a blackout and YES, I answered honestly."

"Well, did you at least have a dream this time? I know you always said it was just darkness in the past." Jay says like he's looking for something to hold on to outside of worry.

"Nope. I did see a bright light though so that's new. Not sure what that means but what can you do"? I answered, somewhat resigned myself.

Shrugging my shoulders, I turn my head to look out the window. I can only imagine what that bright light could have meant. I always wondered what it was like to dream. I would hear friends at school dreaming of boyfriend crushes and new cars, but I couldn't join the conversation. I would just smile and nod my head because I couldn't remember the last time, I had a dream. Seems strange to me. Everybody dreams, right?...

2

Now… I'm Tired

We pull up to the office on 5th street, 20 minutes from downtown, just after 7 o'clock. At least we missed rush hour. That alone, in this summertime traffic, is a miracle. Although the day is gone, seeing the beautiful colors of the sunset stretched across the sky, it's at least peaceful. Breathing in the fresh air as I open the car door does make me feel a little better. Walking into the office, I noticed a few papers that fell on the floor, probably in the haste of getting me to the ER, so I reach down to pick them up before we sit down and turn on our computers.

"Alright, let's pull up the info we have on the case".

As I reach for my notepad, someone knocks on the door. We looked at each other confused. "I'll get it, " I say to Jay.

"NO!! You're supposed to be resting!!" Jay says while giving me the stink eye. This is going to be a long night, I can tell.

"It's Pastor Mark." He says while looking through the peephole.

Oh, Pastor Mark's here. I know Jay goes to Unapologetic Faith Church (UFC) so maybe he's here for Jay. Other than that, I can't see what Pastor Mark would be doing here. It hasn't been that long since we left the meeting. Maybe he forgot some of the details. Did something else happen already?

Jay opens the door to let Pastor Mark in. "Hey Pastor! How are you? What brings you here?"

While Jay is closing the door, Pastor Mark steps further into the office and addresses us both.

"Hey guys. I just came to check on Rya and give you additional information I just received on the break-in. Thanks JC, for calling me earlier to let me know what was going on. I got your text about Rya being discharged and you all leaving the ER. I figured I could catch you both here."

Looking over at me, Pastor Mark asks, "How are you doing, Rya?"

"Aww, do you check on all your investigators or am I special"? I smile with that bright smile I've been giving everyone lately.

"I mean, you cute and all but I'm saved so...."

Pastor Mark stops talking when he realizes my mouth is wide open in shock. Did he just diss me? I mean, I'm saved! Granted, I know Pastor Mark from the neighborhood community events where we help the youth, and we don't run in the same circles. I don't actually go to church either so I guess he wouldn't know that I was saved. Clearly, this isn't the right time or approach to be making jokes about being special when he's trying to be serious. Plus, I'm not interested like that. I mean he is cute, but he's a client! I guess I asked for that one. Dang… That's a new low to get rebuffed by the Youth Pastor. To be honest, I just wanted to make light of my recent situation, but I guess I'll just pick my face up off the floor and focus. Jay is across the room snickering trying not to have a full-on belly laugh at my expense while I'm giving him a look that says, 'You better not laugh at me.' He sobers up once Pastor Mark starts speaking again as if he's stunned. Is Pastor Mark… rambling? Wait, why is he rambling?

"I'm sorry, Rya. I didn't mean anything negative by it. I'm just not looking for anything like that right now. I mean, I know you were playing, I just didn't know how to respond. Can I start over? I honestly did come to make sure you were ok and tell you something I learned about the case. JC told me you blacked out so I was concerned, I mean anyone would be concerned, right? I figured I had information about the break-in anyway so I thought I would come by. I'm sorry if I offended you. Was I out of line? Are you ok? What did the doctor say? I never knew anyone that had blackouts before."

Well... I didn't expect genuine concern. I was going to tease but he seems to be serious. Let me be nice. Haha! After all, he is a Pastor and the contact for my case.

"Well, now that I've picked my face up off the floor, I'm just fine. What do you have for me? I'm all ears".

I smile again to let him know I'm honestly fine. I guess smiling is my new technique of reassurance. Eh, it works, why not? While giving me the piece of paper he wrote the information on, Pastor Mark clears his throat and explains the other reason he came to the office.

"We heard from one of the members that they may know who did the latest break-in. His name is Dante Daniels. Dante used to be a member of the congregation. I don't have his updated information, but I wrote down the member's information who gave the statement. I asked her first to make sure it was ok. Patricia Sanderson is her name. She didn't really want to get involved but indicated, if it helped catch Dante, she was willing to help. I told her I would be meeting with you soon so Patricia's expecting your call."

I thanked Pastor Mark and let him know we'll follow up and keep him posted moving forward. Walking Pastor Mark to the door, I open the door to let him out and lock up behind him. Jay frowns at me for getting up but he couldn't say much because I was walking the Pastor out. (Muahaha)

Turning around as he walks out the door, Pastor Mark says, "I really am glad you're ok, Rya."

"Thank you, Pastor Mark. I appreciate it. Talk to you soon".

After closing the door and locking up behind Pastor Mark, I lean my back against it out of pure exhaustion. What a day. Now, I'm tired.

3

What's With The Blackouts?

Pulling up to my house, my cell phone rings with my mom's number on the caller ID. It's around 9 o'clock so I figured my parents would be calling. Given how anxious Jay was, I'm pretty sure he called my parents with initial information about my blackout and updated them when I was in the ER getting the tests ran. I didn't see him use his phone in the office, so they haven't been updated for at least an hour. Jay, while putting the car in park, sees the name on the face of my phone. He looks up wide-eyed and bids me farewell because he doesn't want to be a part of this conversation. I knew I should have called my parents earlier. See what happens when you think you're grown? You panic before picking up the phone because your parents are calling. I'm in trouble and I now have to deal with it. Waving goodbye to Jay, I open my front door, step in, and lock it behind myself. With the cheeriest voice I can muster, I answer the phone.

"Hey mom! I was just about to call you".

"And what took you so long?! Jay was the only one giving us updates and that's the only reason I didn't bring myself down there!! You left the hospital over an HOUR ago!! Why have we not gotten a phone call, Rya?! We were worried!"

"Mom, I'm sorry. I knew Jay was letting you both know, and I lost track of time once we got to the office. I just wanted to make some headway on the new case".

I knew right after I finished talking that telling my mom about going to the office was a mistake. Why did I tell her that?!

"Rya Mae Jones! Don't make me hurt you!! You are NOT too old for the rod, little girl!"

Hearing his footsteps in the background, I know my father is about to weigh in on the situation.

"What did she do now, Miriam?"

"Rya went to work after being in the ER AND she didn't even have the decency to call us after her blackout! Every text or update came from JC. What if something were to happen to her for real, Jeff!"

My dad sighs before he answers. "Rya, you know I understand the need to get the job done but listen to your mother, okay? You know she's right. We worry when you don't check in, especially after blackouts. You should have gone HOME and worked on the case. That would have been better. I used to bring my work home all the time. Remember that one for next time, ok?"

While laughing I say, "I'll do that. Thanks dad."

I laugh because I know my mom and dad well enough to know he's about to get in trouble for telling me to work. I get my sense of humor and work ethic from him, so he understands. He has a tough time leaving a case unsolved whether new or old. However, when my mom puts on her sweet voice while she's talking to dad, he also knows he's in trouble.

"Honey, you know I love you, right? But you, telling her to go home and work on the case, is NOT helping!"

With an, 'I surrender voice', my dad responds: "You're right Miriam. I'm sorry honey. Rya, listen to your mother, sweetheart. Love you!" I then hear my dad's footsteps decreasing quickly as he makes his exit to avoid any more trouble.

See. This is normally how these conversations are: Mom disapproving of my actions and tearing me a new one. In this case, it's because I had a blackout and didn't do the right thing afterwards. Then dad, coming and telling me he understands, but to listen to my mom. If I don't check in over the next few days with my parents, I'll never hear the end of this admonishment. If my parents even think I may have another blackout, I will have to prepare my guest room because they will be coming over to stay with me for the foreseeable future. I know they mean well so I don't mind, but man it can be challenging sometimes. You would think I wasn't a grown woman.

"Well, Jay just dropped me off at home and I plan to rest as soon as I unwind and get ready for bed. Promise mom."

"Rya, I know they have not or may not ever find anything, but there could be other neurological or psychological issues we can't see yet. I just want to make sure you're not causing more issues by not resting after another unknown episode. These incidents can happen at any time and with you taking on a new case, I don't want to lose you too." Mom says sorrowfully.

Sobering from the indication of what she means, I answer her a little closed off without being disrespectful. "Yes, ma'am. I understand what you're saying, I'm sorry, and I'll do better next time. It's getting late so I'm going to go to bed, mom."

"I'm sorry baby. I didn't mean to bring him up. I just…" She answers in a rush as if she's trying to take back the indication of what her words meant.

"It's ok mom. Of course, I appreciate your concern and understand where you're coming from. I just can't deal with that right now. I'm going to go. Talk to you later, ok?"

Sadly, she says, "Okay baby, glad you feel better. Good night."

After hanging up, I close my eyes and take a couple of deep breaths to hold back the tears. Yep, not going there tonight.

Having a mom who's a psychiatrist, she knows exactly how to get to the heart a matter. She has a hard time letting things go that she can't make sense of. Not having my brother as a buffer doesn't help either. I know she didn't mean to bring him up, but I've had enough stress for one day.

Even though I really want to dive into the case, I agree with my mom and everyone else: I need to relax. I shower, grab a glass of red wine, and pick up a murder mystery because clearly, being an investigator is not enough. Before I even sit down, I know I'm not going to be able to read it. I can't figure out why I had this blackout. It's been almost ten years. What was so significant that caused it after all this time? I need to find the underlying cause of these or how can I do my job? I can't be willy-nilly passing out in the middle of nowhere and still be taken seriously! Or worse, putting myself and others in harmful situations! The only thing that's different this time is me taking the case for UFC. I haven't stepped foot in a church since Lucas was alive. Why would me taking a case about break-ins at a church have anything to do with me having blackouts all of a sudden? That would be crazy, right? I take cases all the time and nothing. No blackouts, bright lights or strange feelings.

If I'm thinking like this, I really do need some sleep.

4

Remember, I'm 'Professional Rya'...

Up, fed, and dressed in my usual black leather jacket, skinny jeans and leather boots, I'm out the door by 7:30a.m. Yes, I'm aware it's summertime, but it's my Batman suit. Yes, leather can be hot, but at least it's midriff. Hopping on the freeway to head toward the office, my phone rings with Jay's ringtone.

"Hey Jay, what's going on?"

"Hey Rya. I need you to come to the church. There's been another break-in attempt."

"On my way."

While on my way to the church, I called my contact, Becky, at the Station to let her know there's been another break-in attempt at the church. She informed me that she would get a patrol car out to UFC as soon as possible to take statements and collect evidence. Becky is the Chief's personal assistant. Chief Donald set it up himself to make sure I had close access to him without going through an added middleman. He took over when my dad retired and assumed because one of my degrees in criminology that I would follow in my father's footsteps. He expressed how he wants me to work for the department, but with all the corruption and cruelty I saw through my dad's experiences, I'd rather be on my own. I don't mind working with them, just not directly under them.

The church isn't too far from my office, about 35 minutes in the opposite direction of my home. Because I had just left the house, I made it to UFC in record time. Arriving at the church, I find Jay at the front door with a camera taking pictures of the damage. Since this will be Jay's first time in the field,

I'm going to let him walk me through the scene and I'll be his guide along the way.

Pulling up to the church, I get out of my car and approach Jay. "I called Becky to send a car out. They're on their way. What do we have Jay"?

"Pastor Mark was here early for a youth event meeting when he heard loud thumps. As he was coming from the back to see where the noise was coming from, he noticed two silhouettes on the other side of the glass inserts in the doors. At that point, Pastor Mark realized someone was trying to break in by kicking in the doors. He yelled 'Hey, I'm calling the cops!' while running to catch them. Once they looked up and realized someone was coming, they ran. Pastor Mark looked at what they were doing once he felt the coast was clear, and saw all the scratches, scraps, and dusty footprints from trying to kick in the doors. He called me when he got back to the office and that's when I called you."

Trying to make sure I remain professional but failing, I asked Jay about Pastor Mark. "So, he decided it was an innovative idea to look without knowing for sure, huh? Why didn't Pastor Mark call me or the police? Where is he?"

"Yeah, I wasn't surprised to hear Pastor Mark say he looked at the damage. He's usually the one telling everyone he can do it himself and probably figured he could handle this too. I'm sure Pastor John made him reminding Pastor Mark that the church hired you to handle this case. He's in his office with Pastor John now. Pastor Mark said he didn't call you because he wasn't sure if you were well."

This is the stuff that makes the job harder, you know. He just has to be extra. On top of the fact that he didn't call me directly, but my assistant, is just an insult. He saw me yesterday. He knew I was well enough to call and respond. Having enough emotional and mental problems running through my mind is making it harder for me to want to remain professional. Pulling myself together as we through the sanctuary, the first door on the left is Pastor Mark's office. Since the door is already open, Jay and

I walk in, say hello to Pastor John, and I address the elephant directly:

"Do you know how dangerous that was for you to check the damage done to the door without having backup? You didn't know if they were truly gone or not. They could have been armed and waiting for you to check where you couldn't see them, especially since they were trying to kick the door in."

He takes a deep breath before he responds. "I know as Pastor John keeps pointing out. I won't do it again but thank God, I'm fine."

"So that's it? You won't do it again? Are you sure about that? Your actions were pretty reckless. I need to know if I should be concerned about whether or not you're going to trust us to handle this investigation."

With an attitude of arrogance, he says, "What do you want me to say? I knew I could take care of it myself, so I did. I'm always strapped. But as Pastor

John informed me, that is not my job. We hired you for that. So yes, I'm sure. Anything else?"

It was my turn to take a deep breath and remind myself that I'm not Rya the civilian. I'm Rya the investigator, the professional. I know how it feels to think you have it all under control. I also understand how Pastor Mark feels when you realize you don't. I remind myself of that before I speak again. Although I heard Pastor Mark's words of no longer handling it, I've heard that too many times before to just take it seriously. Maybe Jay can keep tabs on him. We'll discuss that as an option later. Right now, Pastor Mark is giving me a look that lets me know he wants me to drop it. In return, I give him my 'I'll drop it when I'm ready to' face- which is a sugar sweet smile with a hint of don't mess with me. This is going to be a long case; I just know it. Back to the matter at hand.

"Can you identify anyone? Did you see any details, defining features for a sketch artist that will help us get a good picture of who they might be?"

"No, I didn't get a chance to see anyone's face. By the time I even made it to the door, they were long gone." Pastor Mark replies with a little more saltiness than I care to address.

Entirely over his attitude, I continue. "Alright, do you have everything you need here? I think it's safe to say you should leave for the day. Pastor John is leaving soon, and you shouldn't be here alone anyways knowing there was an attempt so recent. Clearly, this is beginning to escalate, wouldn't you agree, Pastor Mark?"

"Rya… I appreciate what you're saying and what you're doing. I also agree that it seems to be getting worse, but I will not run. They will not keep me from doing what I know I'm supposed to be doing. I hope you didn't just expect me to pick up and leave because you said so. I've been in worse situations than this. I have a youth event to plan. I can hold my own if I need to, whether anyone is here or not."

"Pastor, no one is asking you to hold your own or even to run. I'm also not asking you to just pick up and leave. What I am asking is that you choose to use wisdom in a circumstance where others can be affected by your decision to hold your own. That very mindset could put others around you at risk who might not be able to hold theirs should something unfortunate happens. How about a compromise, Pastor Mark? We have evidence to collect. Jay and I will go and gather some details and information with the police who are on their way. You can finish whatever it is you need to, and we can all leave at the same time. How does that sound?"

Grumbling, he agrees. "Yeah, that's fine. I should be done by then anyway."

"Great! I'll leave you to your work."

Leaving the office, I look over to Pastor John who's clearly amused.

"Pastor John, are you laughing at me? What did I say?"

With a twinkle in his eye, Pastor John says, "Nothing."

He looks back at Pastor Mark with the same expression and leaves the office to go head home. Pastor Mark sees the expression on Pastor John's face, sighs, and gets back to work. Maybe it's an inside joke I don't want to know about. Focusing back on the case, Jay and I head out of the office and walk toward the front doors of the church. We talk through our strategy while waiting for the patrol car to come. Getting to the front door, Jay and I see two of the department officers heading our way. We greet Keith and Adam, give them the details from the attempt, and let them proceed with gathering evidence. Looking at Jay, I catch him staring off into space.

"Jay, what are you thinking? You have that faraway look on your face."

"Well, for one Pastor Mark actually listened to you."

The officers look over at me with a perplexed expression. Shrugging my shoulders and ignoring Jay's answer, we get back down to business.

"Umm ok, anything else?" I say while giving him a look that says pull it together.

Sheepishly, Jay says, "Sorry. The main thing about these break-ins is I feel like they're an inside job. I'm just not sure how yet."

The guys are busy looking at Jay and taking notes over the information he's already relayed to me, so I continue with my question after he finishes speaking.

"What makes you say that?"

"Well, for one, Pastor Mark seems to always be here when they happen, even in the past. That could be a coincidence, but Pastor John seems to be nowhere around and nor are the other Pastors at the time of these occurrences. Given that Pastor John had just arrived when I did, I was able to ask him about the earlier incidents. From what I've been able to piece together, the attempts seem to be centered around Pastor Mark's meetings or day to day work at the church. This gives me the impression that they may know when he's here to even try. Also, why risk breaking in in the middle of the day when it's easier to be caught or recognized? It just feels like there's more going on here than just a few attempted break-ins at a local church, you know." Jay states thoughtfully.

"I know you go to this church so, maybe you're right. However, that's a lot of speculation to prove. We need more concrete evidence like people who can be identified so that we can create a profile for them. If these attacks are centered around Pastor Mark, then they're pretty persistent and at some point, will probably be expecting us to look into that fact. If running is the method they're using to not be recognized, it's obviously working since no arrests have been made for them in the past. This lets me know we need to get to the bottom of this case before these break-ins escalate any further."

Keith, the senior officer says, "This area is known for break-ins. We get called out to this neighborhood all the time. People selling drugs, gang members, and just the typical breaking and entering calls come in on a normal basis. If you can prove otherwise for the church break-ins, then we'll put more officers and resources on it. If it's just a hunch, it's not worth our time. We need more evidence. Keep us posted with any further information Rya. We'll see you guys later."

"Will do. Thanks guys. See you later."

Once they pull off, Jay and I put all the evidence collected in the car and wait for Pastor Mark to lock up the church so we can leave. Back at the office, I call and schedule a time to meet with the witness, Patricia, and research information on Dante Daniels. Speaking to Jay, I lay out a plan of action before meeting with our witness.

"Ok, Jay. So, we meet Patricia Sanderson at 6. Let's see what we can find on Dante in the meantime. In addition to the information needed for

Dante Daniels, let's get some background information on Patricia. I want to make sure she really is a credible witness".

Eager to get to work, Jay responds with, "Gotcha!"

Calling the station to get information on Dante and Patricia's backgrounds, we dig more into the file we received for the case to see if we could begin making sense of the timeline for these break-ins. In addition to our call to Becky, we also inquired about the prints and other evidence collected at the church just this morning. If we could get a hit on the prints from an earlier arrest and the like, maybe we could start making some significant connections. From the files we receive from the police department we tried the numbers under Dante's name to no avail. Deciding to try the address we found on Dante after visiting Patricia, Jay and I call it a day and head out for our interview with our witness. We pull up to Patricia's house at around 5:55, and I talk Jay through the strategy before we get out and go to the door. Since this is his first eyewitness interview in the field, I wanted to make sure he was aware of what would or could happen.

"Ok, so according to what you could pull up, Patricia lives alone, has grown children, and goes to UFC. Anything else I need to know before she gives her statement?" I asked Jay while getting out of the car.

"Patricia's been arrested for shoplifting a couple times when she was younger, but not since her late 20's. She is now in her early 40's and has been going to UFC for the last few years. For the last six months, she has volunteered exclusively for the youth events when I asked Pastor John about it."

"So, Patricia has worked exclusively under Pastor Mark? And it's recent?"

"Yes.," Jay responds.

"So, she might have noticed other things going on that could be suspicious. Alright, sounds good. Let's go."

Knocking, I could hear Patricia making her way to the door. She opens it with a nervous-looking smile and welcomes us in. "Hello Rya and JC, come in and have a seat. Would you like something to drink?"

"No, thank you! We don't want to take up too much of your time. We appreciate you agreeing to meet with us. Jay and I understand you not wanting to be involved but admire your courage to come forward with the information you have. Just came by to get your statement on the break-in you witnessed so we can give you back your evening." I say, trying to reassure her.

She seems to visually relax before commenting. "Of course. I'll help in any way I can. I would hate for something bad to happen to Pastor Mark, you know. He's such a good man."

"Why would you expect something bad to happen to Pastor Mark?" I ask curiously.

"Oh no! I was just saying because he was there during all the attempted break-ins, you know." Patricia says.

"Weren't there others at the church for the meeting you guys were having when this attempt happened? How did you know he was present for ALL the attempts?" I ask.

Putting more emphasis on her words than necessary, Patricia becomes somewhat defensive: "Yes, I was there but he seems to be there ALL the time. Everybody tells him to go home or at least leave together but he always says 'no, I got it. I'll lock up. You all get home. I'll be fine.' Pastor Mark *never* lets anyone help him. He thinks he can do *everything* himself. We're supposed to be a community, you know." Patricia replies with her hand on her hip.

"I completely understand. What can you tell me about the attempted break-in you saw a few weeks ago?"

"Well, the youth staff were in a meeting with Pastor Mark about the youth event UFC is having in at the end of the month and started hearing these scratching noises. Since the sanctuary's main doors were closed and locked, we didn't have any additional lighting in the front of the church. Usually that's how it's done when we don't plan on being in church for a long time to conserve energy. Plus, the foyer is the only area between the doors and the sanctuary so if someone were to come, we could see them. The lights from the sanctuary illuminate the foyer fine at night. I was already on my way to the bathroom so I figured I would go and check it out. Could have been an animal scratching on the door trying to find food or something. Anyways, when I got to the door, I saw Dante and another person on the other side of it. I was going to go let them in since Dante was a member here before, but they left when they saw me. I went back to the sanctuary and told Pastor Mark what I saw and that's when he called Pastor John. Pastor John then called the police."

"Ok. Thank you for that information. I was informed that you help Pastor Mark at the church a lot as well. Have you noticed any other implications of who else could be doing these break-ins aside from Dante? Could you identify the other person if you saw an image of them? Another recent or former church member possibly?"

"I think I could name the other person, but I'm not sure. It was easy to spot Dante because when he looked up, I knew who he was. The other person I can't say. I don't think they went to the church or go there now for that matter. He didn't look familiar. Plus, I was too stunned to see Dante on the other side of the door trying to break-in!" Patricia exclaimed.

"Has anyone else reported seeing Dante for any of the other incidents?"

"Not that I know of. No one really likes to talk about these break-ins or any of the violence in the neighborhood. Most people at the church just try to act like everything's fine. Pastor John must have sensed the tension because we've had church meetings about Dante, the break-ins and what we can do. Pastor John says if you see something, say something. The church's been trying to get the community involved more as well."

Nodding and taking notes, I continue my questioning. "When did you start working with Pastor Mark for the youth exclusively? I was told you usually volunteer anywhere you feel needed but recently you decided to only work under him."

"Oh well, I uh, felt that the youth is where I'm called and that was around six months ago. I just have a desire to help the children grow stronger in their walk with Christ. Since I grew up in this neighborhood, I wanted to contribute. Pastor Mark *seems* to be really passionate about making sure the youth don't end up like him when he was growing up. I simply agree with his *direction*. The youth shouldn't be out here selling drugs and getting into gang related activities."

"Why did you say that about Pastor Mark? Was he involved in gang related activity or drugs?"

Surprised and ready to gossip, Patricia replies with a smirk.

"Oh, you don't know?! That's what he did for *years*! He got *saved* and changed his life. It's his story to tell so I can't give you all the details. Pastor John felt the Lord *led* him to Pastor Mark and the rest is *supposed* to be history."

Seeing that she was starting to get irritated among other things, I stopped my line of questioning and thanked her instead. I need to make some calls to confirm her information.

"Ok, thanks for the information, Patricia. I'm sure the youth are happy to have you helping them out. We'll be in touch."

Getting her composure under control, we stand to make our way to the door.

"Of course. *Anything* I can do to help." Patricia replies with a sweet smile.

Leaving Patricia's house felt all kinds of wrong. Why was she stumbling over her testimony? There also seems to be deep-seated anger or at least resentment toward Pastor Mark. The way she spoke about him was suspicious too. Maybe she's jealous of Pastor Mark's position but maybe not. I'll have to look further into her background to find out why. Something about this witness isn't sitting right. Getting into the car, I wonder if Jay picked up the same thing about Patricia that I did.

"Why do I feel like she's hiding something, Jay?"

"I agree. She's definitely hiding something. I felt this same feeling at the church the other day. Could be a connection. I'll also look into how she interacts with the youth. She seemed to get agitated when she described how Pastor Mark is passionate about them."

"Good idea. Make sure to cross reference her with Pastor Mark. She brought up his safety for a reason. Could be nothing, could be everything."

"Ok, I'll go over everything we gather from Patricia after class tonight. Almost done with my final project! Graduation is in a few weeks. Gotta pass these last three classes so I can get my degree and really help!" Jay said excitedly.

"Yeah, I remember those days! I'm proud of you, Jay! Take your time. I'll make some headway on her statement and keep you posted. I'll check on Pastor Mark too".

After dropping Jay off to his car at the office, he heads to school. Making my way back home to do some much-needed research, I received a message from my mom. I decided I would check the message later so I could collect my thoughts on the case. In my recollection, I get a call from Pastor Mark.

"Hey Pastor Mark, any new information?"

"Someone's been to my house." Pastor Mark says angrily.

"How do you know? Is the door open or are any of the windows broken?"

"No, not that I can tell. I got a letter in the mail with no return address and only my name on it that's been handwritten. The first thing I do when I get home is go straight to the mailbox. Looking inside the mailbox to check my mail, I found that this envelope was the only thing in there. I haven't opened it yet because I wasn't sure what to do. I was going to check myself, but since you chewed me out last time, I thought I'd call you."

I'm investigator Rya, not 'Tell You Off Rya'. This must be my new mantra. Ignoring his salty comment, I replied:

"All right. We don't know if there's fingerprint evidence or any number of chemical elements on or within the letter that's meant to cause you harm so don't open it. Don't touch anything else. Are you in the house now? Was anything tampered with? Even if it seems minor, it matters."

"I haven't made it to the house. I stopped when I saw the letter because I wasn't sure if they went that far. I didn't want to put myself in an unknown position again."

"Ok, good! I appreciate that. Get back in your car, check your surroundings but keep your phone on, doors locked, and the car running until I get there, just in case. Text me your address and I'll check your house when I get there for the all-clear. I'll be there as soon as I can."

Calling for back-up which arrived at the same time I did, Adam, the lead officer, and I checked the house and made sure that everything was locked and closed. Paul, the other officer, stayed outside with Pastor Mark to watch him and keep an eye out. After clearing the house, I let Pastor Mark in and left to grab my kit to open the letter as Adam and Paul say their goodbyes to go and finish their rounds. Once Mark and I were all set, I opened the letter and of course it's typed. *Sigh*, thanks for that. That would have been useful if they were more careless and had handwritten the letter too. Maybe leaving behind a fingerprint or two. You know helping a sister out.

"Let's unfold this letter carefully just in case they left prints or even saliva on the seal. I'll have that analyzed later."

Opening the letter, it reads: "Once a Pusher, always a Pusher. You don't get to leave on your feet. The church can't protect you forever."

Looking over at Pastor Mark's face, I've never seen him so pale. "Are you ok?" I ask.

"Yeah... I think I know what this letter is about." He replies shamefully with his head down.

"I know this isn't the best time but I'm going to need you to explain this to me because if it has something to do with the case, it could make a big difference".

"Ok." He closes his eyes, takes a deep breath and blows it out.

"Do you need anything, water, or something before we get started?"

"No, I'm good."

I pulled out my notebook to take notes, but I did not expect his testimony to be this impactful.

With a dazed expression, Pastor Mark shares his story. "When I was in my late teens, my father was murdered by someone trying to rob him. Because of the neighborhood we lived in, the police didn't take it seriously, so the case was never solved. As a teen without a father, it's easy to get caught up with the wrong crowd, especially when your mom has to work all the time. Tony was the Don at that time and accepted me into his family. He treated me like a son and wanting to please him, I did what he asked. It started off with petty crimes like shoplifting or pickpocketing. I think he was testing me. When he felt like I was ready, he let me slang dope. I honestly was nervous about selling drugs because of the people I knew throughout the neighborhood who were already slanging. Tony convinced me that this was the quickest way to get money to help my mom since she was the only one working to support us. A part of me knew it was wrong, of course, but I didn't have enough influence at the time to push me in the right direction. I started excusing it until I became immune to any wrong feelings at all. My mom could tell something was different because she kept asking me if I was ok. I would just give her a lame answer like I was tired from school, etc. She didn't find out until I was so deep in that she couldn't get me out without getting herself and me killed.

    I dealt in my neighborhood until my mid-twenties. Tony told me that the area was drying up and he switched me to a different location. UFC was not too far away from my new block. I had no problem getting customers in that area because I had made a name for myself at that point as a Pusher. Coming out of one of the stores in the area one day, Pastor John invited me to church. Told me Jesus loved me and had a better plan for my life than the one I was living. Do you know I laughed at him when he told me that? I said, 'If He had a better plan for me, why didn't He show me already?' Pastor John told me to 'come to church and find out.' He planted a seed that day I hadn't recognized at the time. Little by little, things just started happening that didn't make any sense. Customers not coming as often, me running into Pastor John more often and him just smiling at me with no judgment. Tony thought I was trying to play him at one point. I told him I would move to another area, but he just told me to hustle and make his money. It took me months to even work up the courage to go. I now know the Lord was working on me because something had been nagging at me since that first meeting. Finally, I saw the church lights on, and I just decided to check it out. Making sure I wasn't being followed or watched by any of my brothers, I made my way to the church and gave my life to the Lord the same day. The problem was I hadn't stopped dealing and wasn't sure how I would get out of the life.

'Getting out of the family is not simply putting in two weeks' notice. There's no retirement package. You leave the family in death, that's it. So, I prayed and prayed and told God if He meant what He said about my life, I needed Him to physically show me another way. A few weeks later we were preparing to leave bible study. Pastor John pulled me aside and told me that one of the janitors was leaving to move out of state and a job was opening for the position. I told him I was interested and asked what I needed to do to get the job. He told me to just show up and they would train me at church. It wasn't nearly as much as I was making, but it would cover everything I needed it to. I hadn't told him I was praying for this, and I didn't tell him I was still dealing. This was the answer I had been praying for. So, I said yes and spent the next two weeks trying to figure out how to stop dealing without getting killed.

'Well, it turned out I didn't have to. While making the last run I planned to make and telling Tony I was out, I was set up. Somehow, Tony heard that the reason my sales were dropping was because I was at church, and I was trying to get out. He told me that night the only way out was death. I didn't know at the time that he was grooming me to be his second which also pissed off the rest of the family. I remember seeing the hate on their faces when he told me all the potential he saw in me, and I was throwing it away for some Man who isn't even here. I remember him saying '*Jesus ain't never done nothing for you. I did for you. I took you into my family and got your moms out of debt. That was me and this is how you do me?!*' I started to explain myself and he told the family to beat me until I was unrecognizable. The family who I thought was all I had started beating the mess out of me. The first hit came from my left. I don't know what they hit me with; I just remember hearing a deafening ringing in my ear and my legs collapsing from the blow. Before I covered my face to protect what was left of it, I saw Tony leaving with four of his closest henchmen. I didn't take the time to see who was there, but it was at least ten of my so-called brothers beating me to a pulp. I thought about trying to fight back but one of them kicked me in my ribs so hard, I figured it was best to curl into a ball so I could get the least amount of damage as possible. With every kick and blow, I'm wondering where God is now. I changed my life around only to be taken out like this: on the cold concrete ground drenched in my own blood. Just when I thought I was going to die there, I heard sirens in the background. For a moment I figured it didn't matter because the police wouldn't make it in time but then they got closer. The brothers must have sensed it too because they ran before they could finish the job. I was beaten enough not to be able to move but I was still alive. Somewhat conscious, I could hear the police storm the building but still couldn't move. Passing out at some point, I woke up in the hospital, handcuffed to the bed after the surgeon repaired my spine and the doctor stitched my left temple. Once the doctors deemed me stable, I was discharged and released into police custody. The police, trying to scare me into talking, told me that I would never see the light of day again based on the evidence they had on me. The detective in charge of my case told me that the kilo of heroin and the weapon I had on me was enough to put me away for 10 years. The deal, if I gave up the other members including Tony, was that they would reduce my sentence. I refused. What good would that do me if I ended up in the same prison as some of the brothers I just gave up.

'At that point, I was broken and devastated. I was finally trying to do the right thing with my life, and this was what I got for it. My court appointed attorney tried to get the judge to let me go until my trial, but the prosecutor convinced the judge that I was a flight risk. I couldn't believe this was how I was going out. No chance to see my mom for 10 years. Who would help her then? Not to mention, not able to go to church. I was prideful at first and felt like I didn't deserve the hand that was being dealt to me. When I finally got over myself enough to pray, The Lord told me this was for my protection and that it would all work out in the end. That was the hope I had to keep my sanity while I was in there waiting to see what my fate would be. I prayed and read my Word while I was locked up. I changed my prayer from, 'Get me out;' to, 'Have Your way and keep my mom.' I even helped other inmates get saved. I was locked up for 3 months before going to court. My attorney told me that the only thing that the prosecutor could make stick was the drugs I had on me. My bond was set for $10,000 or 2 years. I was prepared to do those two years and knew I deserved to. Two days later, I was told my bond was paid and I was free to go on 21 months' probation. I was floored! I had no idea who paid it until Pastor John stepped out of his car outside the county ready to take me home. I stood there speechless not understanding why he would do something like this for me. With tears in my eyes, I asked my new Pastor why he did it? Pastor John smiled and said I was family and that's what family does. He then told me the church was also helping my mom pay her bills as well through a program UFC has at the church for those in need. I cried my heart out and told the Lord I would do whatever He wanted me to with the new life He gave me."

Fully invested in his testimony, I almost forgot to write the notes needed for the case. I had to clear my throat several times to keep from crying. Pulling myself together, I reply, "Wow, Mark. I never knew you went through all of that. That's a powerful testimony!"

"I agree. The Lord gets all the glory though. He also took care of my boss, Tony. Apparently, one of the neighbors nearby heard the commotion and called the police. The police arrived as everyone was trying to leave the scene. From my understanding, they had been waiting for a way to take down Tony and the whole operation. Everybody had drugs and unregistered guns on their person along with my blood from the assault. They each got five years or more. Tony and the henchmen he left with were the only one that got away and went into hiding to avoid the police. He didn't come looking for me even when I thought he would. About 8 years ago, he was found in his house with a gunshot to the back of his head. He only lived a few blocks from where I grew up. I was told by some of the kids at the church that there's a new Don; I'm just not sure who.

'Since being out of jail, I've worked for the church. By earning Pastor John's trust and proving myself, I moved from Janitor to Youth Volunteer, and now to the Youth Pastor. My mom got saved after she spoke to Pastor John and found out how I turned my life around. I know I've hurt a lot of people in my past. I can't change that. But I've worked hard to change my future and help these kids do the same. These kids around here are basically growing up the way I did. They need someone to stand in the gap for them. The Lord told me that's what He's called me to do. Who better to help them than the one who has walked on the other side and can tell them there's nothing out there for them but death or jail. Jesus can give them life and opportunity. I'm a firm believer in that." Mark says confidently.

"Thank you for sharing. That's truly awesome. I know it must have been hard to share this part of your life. I'm sorry you had to relive that, but I believe this may be connected to the case. Can you write down the areas where you used to deal? That would be extremely helpful."

"Yeah, I can do that right now. Telling my testimony is easier than it used to be. Leaving my past behind and finding the Lord helped me see my purpose more clearly. I can mentor the kids in this neighborhood like Pastor John mentored me and lay out real life scenarios because of my life experiences and now, my knowledge of the Father. I truly do wish there was another path I could've taken to get here but I'm grateful He could use my mistakes for His glory."

"That's really great, Mark. I'm glad He could too. Just a few more questions if you don't mind. Anyone you can think of that would target you because of your past? Any particular area I should focus on more than others?"

"Not sure who would be after me. When I left that life behind, I left everything with it including the people. Haven't seen or spoken to any of them in over 10 years. If the location is a concern, I would say start with the location near UFC first. That's where I started changing and where I was set up. The area around my old home and neighborhood was where I first started out and is the only other block I dealt on. I was very reckless and impressionable then. I really want to get some concrete answers on this case, but I hope it's not because of my past. I've done my best to really leave that life behind." Mark replies with a sad expression.

"I hope not as well. Don't beat yourself up though. You said God is using your past to help others. Trust me, we need your expertise and your experiences in this society. Some of the cases I've seen with adolescents these days make the need for your guidance pretty clear. Besides, we all have our issues. I'm glad you found purpose in yours. I'll get on this first thing. I don't think they tried to break-in, nor do I believe that was their purpose tonight. Searching your home for signs of disturbance and not finding anything supports that. Are you comfortable staying here tonight? We can find you a hotel if you need one."

"No, I'm good. I'm not leaving my house." Pastor Mark said with determination.

"That's fine, just don't be a hero, ok? If you need help, call 911!"

"Will do. Thanks again."

I check my surroundings as I exit Pastor Mark's house. Searching the area around his home and the surrounding blocks, I found nothing suspicious or in need of further investigation, so I headed home. I finally get a chance to check my mom's text message and what do I see? A warning. The message says:

> *'Rya, be careful. Not sure what's going on, but I feel like something bad is going to happen soon. Just wanted to let you know. Love you, mom!'*

Mom, I couldn't agree more. Why would somebody leave a note like that at Pastor Mark's house?

5

Was That For Me?

I dreamed last night!! Ok, so I kind of sorta had a blackout right after I got to bed. How would I know that you ask? Because I'm lying with half my body on the floor while the other half is in my bed. When I woke up this morning, it was the same as when I woke up in the hospital: not aware of where I was and feeling utterly discombobulated. I used to have an affirmation that I would tell myself that my mom helped me work out so I wouldn't feel so bad after a blackout. The wording changes but the *At Least* stays the same:

> *At least, I wasn't hurt. At least, I was home. At least, I'm ok.*

These are the things I try to remind myself of because although it's bad; it could be worse. From bruises to bloody noses, trust me, it has been worse.

Today, it's just a sore arm from where I landed. As good as my affirmations and a lack of injury are, they don't make me feel any better today. They just help me suppress my emotions for the time being. Considering this is the second time I blacked out within a week, I'm at a loss putting what I feel into words. The suppression isn't really working out either, but I'm not allowing depression to have its way with me again. I'm not 16 anymore. I have experience dealing with these and as tough as this is, I need to rely on what I know. So, after peeling myself off the floor, I can feel my arm and ankle throbbing from how I must have landed. My essential goal was to go to the bathroom to clean up first, but my ankle said lay down first. So, at 6am, I lay there contemplating because right now that's all I can do to not be in pain from trying to do anything else. This quiet moment gives me the time to collect my thoughts. I can only assume that these blackouts are happening for a reason. The more I think about it, the more I realize maybe Pastor Mark does have something to do with this. How can a person contribute to a blackout? Am I really that stressed by this investigation that I'm blaming it on a person. That's pretty messed up. Maybe I'll give Dr. Chokmah a call to see if there's anything he can prescribe that might help. My mom might have suggestions too. I need to figure something out soon. I don't want to struggle to do my job in fear that I might blackout later. I know these occurrences don't last forever. So, with that in mind, I take a deep breath and redirect my focus.

Choosing to focus on the best part of the blackout would have to be the fact that I had an actual dream this time. The dream, though brief, was me in a seat. Not sure if it was a chair or a booth because I couldn't see. The scene showed me sitting, looking forward, and paying attention to whatever was being said. I couldn't hear what I was listening to, but I knew it was important because I was completely enthralled. I'm not certain what that means yet but it's progress! From what I could tell, definitely good progress. Wow. I dreamed... Despite everything else, it does feel good to dream.

Finally looking at my phone, I see I've missed several phone calls: 2 from Jay, 1 from my mom, and 1 from Pastor Mark. Jay then decides to send me multiple texts in various stages of panic after I didn't answer his calls:

> 1st text~ 7am: *'Hey Rya, are you up?'*

> 2nd text~ 7:20am: *'Rya, it's 7:20, why are you not answering? OMG! Did you have another blackout? Do I need to come over?'*

> 3rd text~7:30am: *'I'm on my way!'*

Can't I even blackout with a dream without someone being in a panic. To Jay's credit, I'm usually up by 7am and I just had another blackout after years prior to the date so I'll give him a break. I text him back at 7:35am:

> *'I did have a blackout but I'm ok. Tell you about it when you get here. Since you're on your way, pick up breakfast. I'm hungry. Returning Pastor Mark's call. See you in a minute.'*

After texting Jay back, I decided to call Pastor Mark as well. Might as well make my rounds while I make coffee. Picking up on the second ring, Pastor Mark tells me the reason for his call.

"Hey Rya! I'm glad you called back. Pastor John isn't feeling his best today and asked if I would cover him for bible study; I said yes of course. Not leading bible study tonight is not an option- just in case you were wondering."

"Can't talk you out of this at all, huh? Nobody else is available?"

"Not tonight and like I said, I won't run." Pastor Mark says.

"Ok, fine. What time is bible study?"

"Seven, why?" He asks.

"Because I'll be coming with you to keep a lookout. If whoever is trying these break-ins show up, which seems to be the case when you're there, then we might be able to catch them in the act and put an end to this case."

Hesitating, Pastor Mark says, "Oh, ok. That sounds good. I'm usually at the church around 6:30 to let people in and set up. Can you come then?"

"Ok…You sure you're ok? You hesitated. Nothing else happened last night?"

"No, nothing like that. I'm good." Pastor Mark says.

"Ok, I'll be there."

While looking at my phone wondering why Pastor Mark hesitated, Jay lets himself in my first door. Even though I'm happy to see Jay, I'm more excited he brought food!

"Ooh food!" I say excitedly while grabbing the bag from Jay and walking to sit on my couch.

"Rya, what happened? You seriously had another blackout?! Are you hurt?" He says ignoring my food comment completely.

"Jay, I'm ok. Yes, I had another blackout. My arm and ankle are a little sore where I fell, but I'm fine otherwise. I do have good news: I dreamed last night!"

Still not convinced I'm ok, he frowns. "Are you sure? You don't need to go to the hospital? Wait, you had a dream? That's awesome! What was it about?"

While Jay checks my head and sore arm to give me his own diagnosis, I relay the dream back to him and the conversation I had with Pastor Mark. He was just as excited as I was! I thought he was excited about me having a dream, but I guess church is more important.

"You know this dream is lining up with you going to church today. Maybe it's about you finally coming back to church." He says as he eats his breakfast burrito and shrugs his shoulders. "Too bad I have class tonight or I would be there just so I could see if it's true."

Realizing I wasn't ready to address the possibility of going to church for me, I moved on. There's a reason why I haven't been to church but that's a conversation for another day. I'm more interested in figuring out whether or not we'll catch the ones trying to break into the church today knowing Pastor Mark will be there.

"We might be able to solve the question of the mysterious break-ins. If the criminals usually show up when Pastor Mark is there, this may be the lead we're looking for. Don't get your hopes up too high, I won't even be in the sanctuary most of the time while Pastor Mark is teaching bible study. I'll keep you posted though."

After Jay leaves, I decide to skip the office today and just take a much-needed break. Having unpleasant blackouts can be exhausting. Between finishing paperwork, working out, and taking a nap,

6pm rolled around quite fast. Time really does fly when you're having fun. Before parking a block away from UFC, I drove a few streets around the church just to make sure I didn't see anything suspicious. UFC rests on a busy street so parking is sometimes hard to find. Because there is a big lot in the back of the church where anyone could be hiding, I call for backup before checking it out. When officers Jeff and Tyler arrive, we say our hellos and I let them in on what we'll be doing this evening. Finishing our perimeter checks, they both decide to walk to their patrol car while I address Pastor Mark. It's not even 6:30 and he's already here with the lights on. Is he taking this seriously or what?

"Good evening, Pastor Mark. I see you made it here even before the time you gave me. You could have let me know you were going to be here earlier. I would have made my rounds sooner. I'm trying to keep you safe, Pastor."

Taking a deep breath, Pastor Mark responds, "I understand that. I really do, which is why I agreed to this in the first place. I know the church hired you to do a job and I respect that. With that being said, I've only been here a couple of minutes to cut the lights on and saw you drive by, so I knew I was good. I don't need a hero, Rya. I'm very capable of taking care of myself if I need to."

"You just called me the other day because someone had been to your home. Someone accused you of not deserving your position and said that the church couldn't protect you forever. I think that constitutes for more than just being capable, given why they may be after you. With that in mind, let us do a perimeter check inside the church just to be safe. Before you go anywhere else in the building, we want to make sure they're no surprises. They could have been in the building waiting for you, and we wouldn't have known a thing. I also need to let the officers know how long we'll be here. How long is Bible Study?"

Dropping his head in shame, Pastor Mark resigns: "Bible Study is about an hour and a half. We usually have bible study for an hour and then a Q&A after for up to a half hour."

"Ok, good. Most of that time, Jeff, Tyler and I will be surveying the area around the church and inside the church. I'll note the time you're wrapping up and make my way back, so we'll be able to make sure everyone leaves safely, too."

"That works for me. Thanks Rya." Pastor Mark says.

"No problem."

As soon as we wrap up our conversation, someone knocks on the door. I go to open it and it's Patricia. She looks surprised to see me and a little flustered.

"Uh hi, Rya, right?"

"Yes ma'am, how are you, Patricia?"

Stumbling through her words again, Patricia responds: "I'm good. I'm good. I didn't know *you'd* be here. Are you staying for bible study?"

"Why, yes, I am."

"Oh good. That's good. I just came early to see if Pastor Mark needed help setting up before we got started." She says patting her hair down.

"Oh, ok. That's nice. Do you come early for all the bible studies?" I ask curiously.

"Uh well only when I can. I got off work early today, so I thought I'd come and help."

"Oh, that's generous of you." I tell her.

Done with our conversation Patricia says, "Well, it was good talking to you. I'll go find Pastor Mark now."

"Good talking to you too!" Hmm…Do I make her nervous?

Forgetting I haven't called my mom back, I make a point to answer her call this time. If I don't, she'll make sure I hear about it later. Bible Study starts in ten minutes, so I have a little time before everyone shows up. Walking outside away from everyone inside for privacy, I answer the phone.

"Hey mom! Everything ok? I'm working on the case right now."

"Hey Ry! Yes, everything is fine. Just checking in to see if you got my text?"

"Yes ma'am! I got it and I've been alert and extra cautious ever since. I had the same feeling. Anything new? I'm at the church with Pastor Mark for Bible Study."

"Oooh…Bible Study with Pastor Mark? Is this work related or…?"

"Mom! Are you serious? This is completely work related!"

Laughing she says, "Ok, ok. Just kidding. Anyway, are you staying for Bible Study? Whose idea was that? I didn't know you were interested in going. I would have invited you a long time ago."

"It was my idea since Pastor Mark must be here, and the circumstances have made it clear he may be the target and needs protection. No invitation necessary, I'll let you know though when I'm interested."

"Well, we didn't want to make you feel judged or rushed into coming back to church because of us. We've been praying you would come around. We all need Jesus, Rya. This life isn't going to get any easier without Him. I understand you're disappointed with Him not saving Lucas, but He has His reasons. We may not understand them, but we can still move forward knowing He cares.

"I'm sure God does care but I just need a little more time to figure that out. It doesn't feel like He cares. I'm working right now though but I wanted to make sure I answered your call before I forgot to call you back."

"Alright. Call me later. Are you staying for the entire Bible Study?"

"Yeah, I'll be here until Pastor Mark leaves."

"Good, make sure you learn something."

"Yes ma'am. Talk to you soon. Love you mom."

"Love you too baby."

My mom makes it hard for me to hide anything. She knows being at church is hard for me after Lucas's death because I feel like God should have saved him. He saved me. Why save me and not the both of us? This is why I avoided taking cases related to churches. The most I would do were the youth events around the city. The only reason I took this case was because of my family. The fact that my mom is this excited I am at a church says it all. I choose to be here tonight because my client is here and may need protection, that's it or at least that's what I'm telling myself.

Growing up, our family didn't start going to church until I was about 12 and my brother Lucas was 2. I didn't understand why this new lifestyle change was necessary, as my parents put it, but I began to enjoy it. I even remember getting saved at summer camp when I was a teenager. Sometimes it's nice to go down memory lane but right now is not the time. It's time to get back to work and hopefully catch a criminal.

After talking with mom, I met back up with Jeff and Tyler. While I walked around the church checking perimeters, locked doors and windows, the officers did a couple of checks around the block. We met back up so I could let them know if I'd seen anything suspicious and vice versa. After concluding that nothing was amidst, I made my way back into UFC. Upon walking into the sanctuary, I sit in the back, catching the end of the Q&A for bible study.

"To answer your question about John 15:5-8, Jesus is the vine that we, the branches, need to stay connected to. The stronger our connection to the vine, the better the fruit we will bear or produce. What are the fruit? The fruit are the outward manifestation of the life we live in Christ given by the Holy Spirit. Is that life going to be a life in Christ, which is the fruit of the Spirit mentioned in Galatians 5:22-23, or of the world? Are you producing fruit of discord or fruit of love? Fruit of unforgiveness or fruit of peace and long suffering? Fruit of wrath or fruit of gentleness and kindness? The bible tells us that, 'We shall know them by their fruit!' So, prove to be Christ's disciples by the fruit you bear in Him! Amen! Did that answer your question?"

The member replies, "Yes, thanks Pastor Mark."

"Before we pray, I want to make sure that if anyone who is unsure of salvation, or if you're unsure where you're going should you leave here tonight, the doors of the church are open. You can raise your hand and we can pray the prayer of salvation with you. Whether you just want to pray for repentance, Christ is more than willing to forgive. If you just need prayer, we are here for you. With no prayer requests and all hearts and minds are clear, let's pray:

> 'God, my God. The God of my salvation, Creator of heaven and earth, and Lover of my soul, I thank you. You gave me a Word for your children today and I pray You would water the seed You gave me the privilege to plant. Your Word says that it will not return to you empty so I pray You fill that Word rooted in their hearts with more of You. Let it produce the fruit You intended it to. I thank You Father because I know it's already done. It's in Jesus' name, I pray. Amen!'"

Absolutely raptured in the Word and prayer from Pastor Mark gave me a sense of Deja vu. I concluded that this moment was in fact my dream. Jay was right. I felt like he was talking to me. That can't possibly be the case though, right? I'm here to do a job. I just came to make sure my client was safe. I haven't been to church since Lucas passed but that doesn't mean anything. I'm still saved. I don't have to go to church to prove that do I? This is really conflicting. Why is all this happening now? I don't know what to make of this yet, but I still have a job to do. Let me get my head back in the game.

Once the prayer ended, everyone greeted each other and began to leave. I stepped back outside to make sure the people got into their cars and drove off safely. Many people were grateful. Others looked at me like I was losing my mind. I guess the police and I looking after them is a foreign thing. Pastor Mark waited for all the members to leave before locking up. I checked the area again to make sure we were not being watched or followed. At that point, I told the officers everyone else was gone and we were fine walking to our vehicles. Jeff and Tyler said their goodbyes and told me to call if we needed anything else. Walking Pastor Mark to his car which was in front of the church, I questioned and commended him on Bible Study. Well, at least the part I heard.

"How was Bible Study, Pastor Mark?"

He responds with excitement. "It went well! I love John 15! It's a constant reminder of the importance of what we do. All the choices we make matter but most important, they matter in Christ. Where the choices I made before Christ would have led me to my death, choosing Christ gave me life. I can't imagine life without Him now."

"Yeah, your answer to John 15:5-8 really has me thinking about the choices I make or made in the past. Do you really believe that it matters to God that much? I mean, it's my life, right?"

Pastor Mark looks at me as if contemplating my question. "But is it? If you gave your life to Christ, it's now His life through you. Your wants take a back seat to His will. That's not always easy to accept but the fruit of it is worth it. I told you my testimony. My life would not look like it does, had I given into the things I wanted even when I was reluctant." He said with a nod of his head like he's confirming his answer as he speaks.

"You've given me a lot to think about. I always thought I could live my life the way I wanted to but be considerate of what the Bible says. Since we're on the subject, I do have a personal question. When you said you came to UFC for the first time and got saved the same night, what did Pastor John say to make you change?"

"I'm glad The Lord is piercing your heart to the point of curiosity. I pray He meets you where you are. To answer your question, Pastor John was actually teaching on this very passage of scripture when I came in that day. He waited until everyone else left before asking me,

> 'At the end of your life when you're getting ready to leave this earth, what type of legacy will your fruit produce? Would people be able to learn and grow from it or just follow your footsteps, be lost, and perish?'

'Those words changed my life. Before we left that night, I gave my life to Christ. I didn't want the kind of life I had to begin with. I definitely didn't want to influence anyone else with how I was living. If there was a better way, then I'd be willing to try it and I'm glad I did." He says with a reminiscent smile.

As Pastor Mark and I get closer to his car, I notice a dark colored car parked a block away in the direction of the church with the lights on. I made sure Pastor Mark was in his car and ready to pull off. Before I could even think to head in the direction of the car, they made a U-turn and left. Yep, it's time to crack this case. Something else is going on here.

Leaving the church, I had to question what my legacy would look like while I drove home. Is it the one I want to leave? I lead a fairly good life, but I always sensed something was missing. Maybe I need to investigate my own life. As I'm contemplating what I should do, I started feeling this strange sensation that I've never felt before. It reminded me of having an out of body experience. Since the blackouts started happening again, I had a thought that this sensation might be a way to warn me. Since I was pulling into my driveway, I had time to grab my things rather quickly and make it into the house in under 2 minutes. Upon feeling faintish, I headed toward the couch to sit down and collapsed instead.

This dream took place on a couch somewhere. Man, that couch looks familiar. But…why am I crying- no sobbing! What kind of dream is this? I'm not even sure how to take this one. While trying to decipher where I am or what the dream was about, it dissolves in darkness, and I wake up.

When I came to this time, I woke up in a cold sweat. Looking around, I see I made it to the couch. Because my blinds were still open, I could tell it was morning so at least I slept all night. Taking a few deep breaths, I slowly allow myself to ponder the details of the dream I just woke from. Being one to not usually have dreams, this was pretty unsettling. What am I supposed to take from this dream because it makes no sense. Coming out of my foggy mindset, I see my phone light up on the floor from my scattered purse. I crawl groggily to discover it's Jay.

"Hey Jay. What's up?"

"Ry, you sound horrible. Stayed up too long after bible study? I know that Word was good."

"No Jay, I had another episode, but a dream came with this one too."

Sounding frantic, he asked, "Do you need me to come over? Do you think you should go to the hospital Ry? That's three within two weeks!"

"Dr. Chokmah's office already reached out and told me they can't find anything so he doesn't want to prescribe me with medication just so I can say I'm taking something. There's a study coming up in a few months for those dealing with sleep apnea and he's recommending I sign up. He's trying to rule out some things so we can get to the bottom of this. I signed up yesterday."

Taking a deep breath, he finally sounds relieved. "Awesome. Ok. I'll let you tell me about the dream later. Get dressed and meet me at the office, I found one of the connections we've been looking for."

I'm usually up and out the door within 30 minutes. It took me over an hour to get ready since I was still fatigued from passing out last night. Pulling up to RJ Investigation Agency, I grab my phone, keys, and purse as quickly as possible and walk through our front office door. Jay brought donuts and coffee so I didn't need to stop. I'll eat real food later. Plus, I really want to know the information he's found.

"Ok Jay, I'm here. What do we have?"

"Remember how Pastor Mark gave us the two neighborhoods where he used to deal and live? When I first cross-referenced Pastor Mark's living residence with Dante, I didn't get anything. So, I cross referenced the areas where Pastor Mark dealt with Dante and got a hit. Curtis Dante Daniels not only lives a handful of blocks over from where Pastor Mark used to deal but he was arrested a month ago and released shortly after for possession with the intent to sell. Dante's a drug dealer, Ry. I pulled up his criminal record and can date his dealing back for more than 10 years. Even if he did go to church for a brief time, he never stopped dealing. From what I was able to gather from Dante's expunged records, he seems like a big deal."

Intrigued, I asked, "Why is that?"

Jay, utterly focused on reading and typing away, says, "Looking over Dante's records, he's had some serious alleged criminal charges, such as assault with a deadly weapon, but was acquitted every time."

"Pastor Mark quit around 10 years ago, right? I wonder if he knows Dante or remembers him. I'll have to ask him about that. I know you wouldn't know Dante since he left before you started going to UFC."

Still determined to give me all the information, he ignores me and keeps going. "You also mentioned I should cross reference Pastor Mark with Patricia, and I got another hit. Patricia lives only a couple of blocks from where Pastor Mark first started dealing as well and has lived there all her life. Her sister Lisa, who is now deceased from a drug overdose, died about 4 years ago. Not sure if that's relevant yet but I have a few more leads to follow. We might need to talk to Patricia again with this latest information to get sufficient clarity."

"Well, the youth event is this weekend. I'll see if there's a time, I can pull her aside to ask a few questions. Great work Jay."

Smiling, Jay says, "Thanks Ry."

Before I can ask Patricia anything, I need more information from Pastor Mark.

6

The Discussions

After calling Pastor Mark about having a meeting involving the case, we pull up to his house. He's already at the door as Jay and I step out of the vehicle.

"Hello Pastor Mark, how are you this evening?"

Looking sober minded, he says, "Doing pretty good. Ready for real answers so we can move forward, you know?"

Nodding at him with empathy, Jay and I walk into the house and take a seat on the couch.

"Yes, I do. That's why we're doing everything we can to get to the bottom of this. We called this meeting because we have uncovered some new information and have a few questions. Do you know who Dante is?"

"Well, he did look familiar when he first came to church, but at that time, I couldn't place him. I thought maybe he was someone I grew up around, but I wasn't completely sure. I only remember all of this because back then Dante approached me about how I got my job and let me know that he was new to the church. He ended up doing the same janitorial work for a little while and then told us he had found a better job elsewhere. Shortly after that, maybe 6 months or so, Dante left the church completely. I figured he just moved on and hadn't thought about him since."

"Around what time did he come to the church? Do you remember?" I asked.

"I would say about a few years after I joined the church which was after I got back from jail."

"Did you ever feel suspicious of him at all? I mean, no offense but you dealt drugs and so you would know what someone from the streets would look like or even act? Did you ever assume his intentions weren't right?"

Giving me an admonishing look, Pastor Mark speaks. "Being from the streets, I will always look at others with an extra layer of caution. But Rya, I try not to judge people for how they look or even appear. My goal is to see the best in others vs always going for the negative. When Dante first came, I knew he was a street dude, but he seemed to be seeking change in his life. He reminded me of myself which was why I looked past everything else. Why are you asking?"

"Well, we have reason to believe Dante had been selling drugs for as long as you were and still is. According to the records we've found, he was a nobody with petty offenses and went to jail at the same time as you. Dante ended up serving his time which was two years. In the last few years, we've seen more serious charges like assault with a deadly weapon or battery charges that don't stick. We believe he may be the new Don. There seems to be a crime and legal trail dating back to about 8 years." I say to Pastor Mark.

"What do you think this means? Did I lead the family to UFC? Am I putting the church in danger by being here?" Pastor Mark questions, sounding alarmed.

"We don't have all the details yet but just wanted to give you this new information to make you aware of what's going on. No one is blaming you for anything and I need you not to blame yourself. I don't want to speculate. We are trying to solve this case and we must follow every lead that presents itself to get to the answers. Just take a deep breath, ok?"

"Ok." Pastor Mark says.

After taking a deep breath, he opens his eyes, looks up at me and nods letting me know he's ready to continue.

"I have one more question for you. How much do you know about Patricia?" Looking over at Pastor Mark, he looks angry and ready for war.

"She's involved, isn't she? I knew it!" He exclaims, getting off the couch.

"Remember, we're not jumping to any conclusions, just trying to piece together the facts. Can you sit down and answer the question please?" I say calmly.

Collecting himself and sitting down, he supplies, "Yeah... Patricia works at the church volunteering for different events or wherever she can help. I don't know much about her past though. She did ask me out a couple of times, but I told her I wasn't interested in casual dating. That's about it. Does Patricia have something to do with this?!" Pastor asks looking a bit hurt.

"We're not sure yet, but anyone could be a suspect. She also lives a couple blocks over from where you used to deal in your old neighborhood.

Her sister was heavy on drugs and died of an overdose a few years ago. How long has Patricia been a member at UFC?"

"About a few years or so. Patricia volunteered with the ministry doing other things at first, but in the last six months, she started volunteering with the youth exclusively. Patricia said she felt like that's where The Lord was leading her to be. The youth department welcomed the help. She recently asked to be my assistant. Since Patricia had been a faithful member, I didn't see the harm in a trial run to make sure it was a good fit." He responds, looking between Jay and I trying to decipher where this is going.

I look over at Jay and he's giving me the same look I'm giving him. Help? Yeah, I'm sure that's what she was thinking.

"So, you allowed Patricia to do a trial run to be your assistant. Can you be more specific on what a trial run means or what that looks like day to day? How recent was this? What have you given her access to?"

"This was 3 months ago. I gave her access to the calendar on my phone so she would be able to keep me updated with appointments at the church. Patricia's involved, isn't she? Patricia asked to gain access to me. That's how they always know when I'm at the church regardless of if someone else is there. Then what does Dante have to do with this?"

I chose not to answer but let Pastor Mark get his frustrations out and calm back down. Once I could tell he was settled, I asked my final question. "Could be nothing, could be everything but I have one more question. I know the church has had these break-ins over the years but recently there's been an influx of calls to the police about more of these attempts happening than before. Can you remember when the more recent break-ins started increasing?"

Pastor Mark stands and begins pacing like he's trying to calm himself down before he speaks.

"The influx of break-ins, whether attempted or successful, started about a couple of months ago. Initially, the church thought the crime was just going up in the area, but we spoke to the residents who go to UFC, and they hadn't noticed much of a change around their neighborhoods. Not saying crime was nonexistent; but it wasn't any worse either. The recent crimes, from what we could figure out, were centered around UFC. So, this is about me? If this Dante character is in fact the new drug lord and knows that I was once in the family, he wouldn't just let that go. You saw the letter, Rya. He's just being strategic. So, Patricia's in bed with the family? I thought you said her sister died of a drug overdose. Why would she want to get involved with them?!"

At this point, Pastor Mark is understandably upset. Although I understand why, I want to make sure we diffuse the situation before he does something irrationally.

"First thing is, I need you to calm down so you can think logically and know that we are here to help you. Secondly, I need you to disconnect her access to you. If she's not involved, this can help us rule her out. But until we know for sure, no one should have access to your direct location unless we can verify that they're not involved first. At least until we solve this case."

"Ok."

Pastor Mark opens his phone, disconnects the link to Patricia, and looks up at me with angry determination in his eyes. I might have to keep an eye on him. I'm not sure what that look means.

"I brought this on myself because of my past. The family's trying to get to me by coming after the church. They sent me that letter too because the people at church are the only ones with my address. I'm trying to live a better life and the family just keeps trying to drag me back down with them! Nobody will drag me back there!"

"Mark, please calm down. The family's not dragging you anywhere. That's why Jay and I are here. We still need to confirm whether this is true. From what we have gathered, the break-ins do seem to be related to your past. But Mark, that is not who you are. You don't want the family to drag you down, then don't let them. Whether it's through drugs or anger, you have a choice, remember that." I look at him pleadingly.

Pastor Mark takes a deep breath, closes his eyes, lets it out, and looks up at me. Nodding with acknowledgement, he says, "I won't. Thanks, Rya."

"Anytime, Mark. Now, are you ok? Do we need to call Pastor John or someone to come and stay with you? I don't want to leave you alone if you're not ok?"

"I'll call Pastor John. He wants to catch up anyway. We haven't been able to meet up much since the investigation started so I'll make my way over there."

Leaving Pastor Mark's house, Jay and I sat in the car waiting for him to pull out of his driveway. At that moment, I had a very sobering thought about Lucas. I thought about all these years that have passed since Lucas's death. That I had buried how I felt about the accident. Hearing Pastor Mark's testimony and how his life is unfolding because of his past, is making it clear that you don't just get over your past issues. You must work through them. Once we set off for the office, I figured it was time to talk about and acknowledge my own past. Who better to start the conversation with than Jay?

We arrived at the office but before we got out of the car, I wanted to have this conversation while I had the courage to.

"Can we talk for a minute, Jay?"

"Yeah, of course. What's up?" Jay replies.

"You know, this case has been causing me to look at my own life: to gain a different perspective on things that I've spent so much time ignoring or denying. I was so upset at first when I started having these blackouts after so long, but I think there's a greater purpose for them. I'm just not sure what that is yet."

"So, what are you thinking? Are you going to talk to your parents? See if they can help you?"

Jay knows if I'm going to talk to anyone to work out my issues, it's my parents. Besides him, they're my best friends. We talk about everything.

"Yeah, real soon. I think it's time to clear the air about some things. That message about fruit with Pastor Mark has been making me think about the choices I've made at least in the last ten years. Would this be how Lucas would have wanted me to live? What would he say to me if he saw me living this way? I thought I was living a good life. Investigating this case has me thinking otherwise."

"It'll be ok, Ry! I'll be praying for you." He says sincerely.

"Thanks Jay. For some reason, I have a feeling that figuring my life out and solving this case will go hand and hand…"

Ready or not, here it comes.

7

I'm Not Ok

The youth event, which I hoped Pastor Mark would have at least postponed given the circumstances, is going off without a hitch. I've been here since 10am when the church volunteers started setting up. A patrol car that I'd called for the event has been driving around the area just to make sure there aren't any issues. This feels like the calm before the storm because I've been on edge since this morning. So far, nothing has occurred. The only suspicious thing that has happened is Patricia not showing up; even though I was told she was supposed to be here. After speaking with Pastor Mark, I tried calling her with my phone and his. Still, no response. I even tried using the church phone and yet no answer, only voicemail. If Patricia wasn't involved in all this, she surely looks guilty. While watching the surroundings, I've also been keeping an eye on Pastor Mark. He looks like he's having a hard time, even though he's trying to enjoy himself.

"Pastor Mark, are you good?"

Sighing he says, "I'm trying Rya; I really am. I just don't know how to act when what's happening with these break-ins is my fault. Almost like there's something else I should be doing to make it right, you know?" Pastor Mark response.

"What do you call what you're doing now? You can't erase your past, Mark. All you can do is pray, ask for forgiveness, learn from your mistakes, and allow God to set you on a path to heal and help others not do the same thing. Wasn't it you who just taught about the Fruit of the Spirit and bearing good fruit in Christ about a couple of weeks ago? Mark, follow your own words. Go back and read your notes if you must but listen to the Word of God. He can help you better than anyone, right?"

Pastor Mark gives me a side eye.

"What?" I ask.

Looking at me with an expression I can't quite make out, Pastor Mark says: "I just didn't expect you to say that. Sometimes you just need a reminder from someone you can trust, that's all."

He smiles. "I needed that. Thank you."

"Anytime." I smile back.

After talking to Pastor Mark, I got back to work. Walking around the lot and seeing the kids have a good time playing games brought a smile to my face. Lucas loved kids. I know he would have been a tremendous help working with them. Maybe I should consider helping; I enjoy working at localized events to help the community. I never thought about helping in a church.

As the youth event proceeds, I continue doing my perimeter checks. Because the function is in the back of the church where the lot is, I make my way around to the front. Pastor Mark said this gathering should only last around 4 to 5 hours, so I make note of that and divide my time between securing the front of the church and watching the back. Since the event ends at 8 and it's 7:55, the patrol officers blow their horn and wave goodbye before driving off for the night. There were no disturbances or any indications that something might take place, so they felt safe enough to leave. As the officers drive away, I begin my final check. As I'm making my way back from the front of the church, I round the corner to head back to the event where the staff should be getting ready to pack up. Based on the laughter I'm hearing from the kids; it doesn't sound like they plan to leave anytime soon. Mindful of my surroundings as I'm walking, I look back and notice a car on the street behind me with their headlights on. Nothing unusual about that so I take heed of it but keep going. Almost to the corner, I can hear the sound of crushed concrete behind me as if a car is moving. Turning back again before I turn the final corner, I notice the same car driving slowly towards me. I turn the corner but keep watching the vehicle out of my peripheral to see what the intention of this slow-moving vehicle is. Suddenly, I have this feeling of doom that comes over me almost like a warning. Instead of walking off into the middle of the festivities and clean-up crews, I stayed at the corner to observe them out of their line of sight. As I'm eyeing the car, the interior lights come on as if they're adjusting and can't see without them on. Squinting to see if I can make out what's going on, I see the outline of what looks like an automatic weapon. Following my instincts, I stay to verify what I unfortunately suspect is happening. As the back driver side window rolls down, I run toward Pastor Mark and shout as loudly as I can, "GET DOWN!! SHOOTER!!"

Everything felt like it happened in slow motion. Pastor Mark, who was so stunned based on his stocked still position, snapped out of it once I shoved him to the ground. The sound of gunfire seemed like it went on forever. But it was hearing the screams of the children that caused me to run after the car to try to get the license plate number. While calling for the police with the license plate information, I saw Dante stick his head out of the driver's side and look at me to make sure he knew I saw him but also to let me know he saw me. The shooter, who I didn't know, stuck his head back in the back driver side window while they drove away rather quickly. Giving the 911 dispatcher a description of the vehicle, Dante and the license plate number, I asked for an ambulance in case there were possible injuries and casualties. After making sure that was taken care of, I went to check the adults and children. I needed to make sure everyone was ok and how I could help. I found Pastor Mark after the ambulance arrived to make sure he was ok. I find him checking on people with that decided glint in his eyes again.

"Pastor Mark, are you good?"

"Yeah. Just making sure the kids are ok."

Knowing how he responded the other day when we told him about Dante and Patricia, he's a little too calm for me to be comfortable. Because the ambulance and police are still on scene helping people, I don't have time to address his demeanor right now. I give the police officer my statement and help them take statements from other witnesses. Once the last of the children left and the police were putting down markers and photographing the scene, I asked Mark again how he was feeling.

"Mark, are you sure? I don't want to bother, but you're a little calmer than I thought you would be after something like this." I ask with my hands out in a calming position. I don't want to escalate the situation, but I don't want any additional incidents on my hands either.

"Rya, this drive by is on me. These people wouldn't even be bothering UFC if it wasn't for the fact that I'm here! But I plan to make it right. I can't let these kids get hurt! They had nothing to do with Dante or anybody! This is between me and the family!"

"What do you mean, 'You're going to make it right, Mark?' Do you plan on going after the family?

Choosing to change means you don't live that life anymore, remember? You told me nobody would keep you from doing what you were called to. Think Mark! Going after them is not the answer for this drive by."

After looking in the direction the vehicle drove in for a few minutes, Mark finally looks at me, and walks off without speaking. He walks toward the front of the church without speaking a word to anyone. Since the police officers were taping off the area, I let him go and went back to see where I could be of use for this new turn of events within the investigation. Making sure the police were finished and able to leave myself, I made my way to the front of the church as well. Waving to the officers for a second time, they all leave. All that's left now is police tape and bad memories. Looking at the lot which held so many peaceful functions made me think about his bible study message again. How will my fruit look when they come into fruition?

Doing one more perimeter check before leaving, I make my way into the church to find out who's still here because there's a light on in the front and the front door isn't locked. I find Pastor Mark on his knees in front of the altar with his head down. Not meaning to eavesdrop, I hear his prayer anyway:

"Lord, I don't know what to do. I've given you my life, and my past is still here reminding me of who I was and what I did. You let them come after the kids today. I know Lord, that You have a plan but Lord I'm having a hard time believing this is it. I mean, these were kids! I'm just supposed to sit back and let the family get away with this? Who will get justice for them? Who will let Your children know that they're protected? I need a sign, Lord, that I'm not supposed to be who I was to get the job done."

Walking forward, I give a response. I'm pretty sure this isn't the one he was looking for because I'm not God, but I feel like he needs to hear this anyway. Maybe it is from God.

"Mark, this is not your fault. I understand it feels that way, but you didn't make the choice to shoot up a youth event today. Yes, the life you used to live may have made the family feel like they had an obligation to show you who's boss, but who is your boss? If it's your old crew, then I understand your need for vengeance; but if it's the Lord, then I'm pretty sure that 'getting the job done' is not the route He wants you to take." I say pointing to the podium.

Stepping up next to him, I get on my knees too. This moment felt too important to leave him here alone. He leans over and places his head on my shoulder. I just smile and look forward. Being here at the altar, on my knees in a position of submission, brought back a flood of memories. I realize that I needed this, this submission and acknowledgement of The Lord, just as much as Mark did. Christ was just waiting on me to reach for it, for Him.

We sat there for a while before Pastor Mark said he wanted to call it a night. He felt like he was ok and was just ready to just go home. While Pastor Mark locked up and left the church, I waited. Having a sudden moment of clarity, I knew what I had to do. There was no way I could keep talking to Pastor Mark about this case or the drive by not being his fault, but not deal with my own guilt.

Following that train of thought, I headed to my parents' house once I left the church. It was time I talked to my parents about Lucas. Pulling up to their home after briefing them on what took place at the church, I was ready to have this long overdue talk. I took a deep breath because I knew this would be hard. I hadn't talked about the accident which ended in Lucas's death in ten years. I didn't see it being any easier now, but at this point, I know I can't keep putting this conversation off like the feelings or the thoughts will go away. After what happened today, I wouldn't want to leave this earth knowing it was something I was supposed to do and didn't. Getting out of the car and walking up to the front door, I let myself into the house and made my way to where I knew my mom was watching TV in the Living

Room. Looking up at the ceiling just before entering the Living Room, I say to myself, God, if You're listening, I really need your help right now.

Entering the Living Room from the Kitchen, my mom sees my face and her expression shifts from a smile to somberness.

"Rya, you don't look so good. I know you told me you were ready to talk on the phone, but I don't want you passing out on us. Are you sure? You can rest first before we talk. We have all night."

"No, mom. I'm sure."

Coming into the living room, my dad asks, "Hey Rya, sure about what? What's wrong, sweetheart?"

"She's ready to talk about Lucas, Jeff..." My mom says to my dad with concern.

My dad, now looking the same way my mom is, takes the same approach she did: "Baby girl, we can talk when you're ready. We won't rush you."

"After the dreams I've been having and what happened today, I can't keep making the excuse of not being ready. If I want to grow, if I want to bear good fruit like the Word says, then I need to get rid of the toxic things in my life that are causing me to produce bad fruit. I've not been growing. I've been dying…slowly, because I was afraid to let go. It's time I talk about happen with Lucas."

Mom scoots over on the couch and pats the seat next to where she's sitting, as if I'm fragile. Maybe I am. My dad takes the other seat next to me so I'm sitting in the middle of them. Collecting my thoughts as I sit next to my mom and dad, I feel protected and raw at the same time. I look around the room and my eyes land on the last family picture we ever took while Lucas was alive. We haven't taken one once. It wasn't the same…

Reflecting on the day, I start at the beginning of the story that led to the accident. "We were arguing in the car on the way home. That's the first thing I remember. Lucas wanted to stay at the mall longer because his friends were there. There was this girl he liked and got mad because I made him leave. I had to get back home because I had just gotten the information for a new case, and I needed to look it over. Lucas didn't want to hear it. The only thing he knew was that he couldn't impress his potential girlfriend and needed to let me know. I told Lucas that he could do whatever he wanted to with his own license, but until then he had to do what I wanted him to. I think I embarrassed him in front of his friends because then Lucas told me I wasn't a good investigator anyway so what was the point? It hurt to hear him say that even though I knew he didn't mean it. At that point, I got angry and said Lucas wouldn't pass his driving test anyways because all Lucas thought about was those stupid girls. I told him those girls didn't like him; they just liked his status. At that point, Lucas shoved my arm and I had to jerk the car back over to make sure we didn't run off the road. I was yelling at that point and wasn't paying attention to my surroundings. That drunk driver came out of nowhere. One minute I'm telling Lucas not to ever do that again and the next, the car is flipping and we're screaming for a totally different reason. I couldn't hear Lucas over the sound of my own heart, but when we stopped moving, I knew he was badly injured. I tried calling his name, but Lucas didn't respond. His face was so bloody, and my eyes were blurry so I couldn't see if he was awake or not. All I knew was he hadn't moved. A part of me knew Lucas was gone but I just didn't want to accept that. I cried out to God not to take him, but to take me instead. I didn't want to end it like that. I wanted another chance to say I was sorry and that I loved him."

While retelling this entire incident, I'm crying. I look up to see my parents crying as well. I look down at my hands so I can make sure I finish getting this out. If I don't finish now, I probably never will. Trembling, I continue.

"I know you guys didn't blame me but looking at so many faces while in the hospital, I couldn't help but blame myself. People coming to see you to express their condolences but looking at you with pity and a bit of anger. Nobody was angrier at me than me. I'd already been an investigator. I knew better than to let myself get that upset and distracted behind the wheel. Would the outcome have been different if we weren't arguing or at least if I controlled my anger? Was there something else I could have done differently? Maybe not, but knowing I was the one driving didn't make me feel any better. I thought about going after the drunk driver. I'm an investigator, right? My dad was the police chief. I had the skills and resources to easily get the information I needed for my own form of vengeance, but I was the only survivor. People told me I was lucky to have survived. It doesn't feel like I survived. It just feels like I'm here going through the motions."

At that point, I couldn't talk anymore. The sobs just wouldn't stop. I spent all these years feeling like I killed my brother. Like because I was the one driving, I was the one responsible for his death. The hurt, anger, guilt, all the shame just felt like it would suffocate me. Just when I felt like I couldn't take it anymore, I felt arms come around me, both physical and internal. This hug felt like an overwhelming sense of comfort that I've never felt before. It calmed me in a way I didn't know was possible, that I couldn't explain. Confessing my thoughts to my parents and this wonderful embrace is the first time I felt like I could breathe freely in ten years. When I was calm enough, I spoke again.

"I don't want the accident to be the way I remember Lucas. I want to be able to talk about him without guilt. If Lucas were here, he would be looking at me like I was crazy for saying that." I chuckled.

We all laugh through the tears because we all know it's true. Lucas was one of the most optimistic people I knew. He would not want us wailing in guilt over him and I'll have to remember that. Knowing I'm somewhat ok, my mom helped me understand how they have been healing.

"Rya honey, we don't have all the answers but one thing we can say is the accident was NOT your fault. Yes, you both were arguing, and you could have been more alert; but you weren't the drunk driver who ran a red light that day. You didn't decide to get behind the wheel knowing your thinking was impaired, erratic, and irrational. People have a choice. You have to choose to forgive and release all of this to Christ. This is not letting go of your brother's memory, but this is letting go of the hurt, anger, and guilt that comes along with it. The Bible says to cast our cares on Christ for He cares for us. Jesus loves you just like He loves Lucas and He cares, Rya. Dad and I know because we've been through this. He's shown us that moving forward is possible and The Lord sent us people to help comfort and support us in this process of healing. God sent us to a church where we could get the Word in an unapologetic way to help us learn His ways and grow in our relationship with Christ. It doesn't bring Lucas back, no. However, I'm comforted in knowing Lucas is with Christ and I will see him again. The Lord may not have kept Lucas with us here on earth, but He did save Lucas that day. The Lord just decided to take him home instead."

Hearing my mom speak while crying, I finally have a revelation. This was the dream I had where I was sobbing on that familiar couch. The Lord meant for me to be here. It was meant for me to deal with the weight of Lucas's death. It was meant for me to be free so I could move forward to produce the good fruit the Bible was talking about. Before I could articulate any of that to my parents, I blacked out.

This dream felt different because instead of feeling like I was watching the dream take place; it felt like I was actually there. The dream opened at a crossroads. Instead of the crossroads being three roads, it was two with a multitude of trees surrounding each path. The first path was wider than the other. The trees on the first wider path had fruit on them in distinct stages of decay. Stepping closer to the first path, I could see that some of the fruit had fallen off the trees around them. Those fruit on the ground were completely rotted out like pulp. What intrigued but horrified me at the same time, was that the decaying fruit was still attached to the trees. In fact, when I looked closer, they seemed to be visibly rotting at different stages of spoilage while on the trees. I concluded that the trees themselves, which are supposed to give life and nutrients to increase life, were sucking the life out of the fruit on them. With undeniable revulsion, I stepped back from those trees and looked at the other trees connected to the other path. I found the exact opposite. Though all the fruit were not completely ripe, they seem to be in various stages of growth, of vibrance, of life. These were also still hanging from the trees. There was one significant difference outside of the life on these trees: None of the fruit on these trees had fallen on the ground. None were overripe. None were dull or lackluster. None were dying.

Immediately, I remember the words that have been playing in my head since that bible study, 'What type of fruit will your legacy produce?'

I cried out, "Lord, I want to produce good fruit! I want to do it the way You want me to, but how do I do that?!"

As I was speaking the dream started to fade. "No! Lord, I'm sorry! Please tell me what to do!!" Before I came to, I could have sworn I heard in a whisper the word 'Choose.'"

8

Revelations

Going into the office today seemed pretty significant. Since Jay was one of Lucas's friends and my stand-in little brother, I thought it was important to also share with him the conversation I had about Lucas. Jay was pulling up when I arrived. Going into the office, we continued as usual. Jay opened his laptop while I sat there for a moment collecting my thoughts before I spoke.

"Jay, this investigation has me thinking a lot about my past. Seeing Pastor Mark's past unfold before our eyes is forcing me to see how decisions from the past can affect the future before we even get there. I know I've been reluctant to talk about Lucas because it's just too painful to relive; but between the dreams, Bible Study, and Mark's life, I know I need to. I just don't see why church is the answer to that."

"Ry, church is not the answer, Jesus is. Yeah, going to church is a part of fellowshipping, learning, and growing but going to church is not just about that. Christ wants a relationship with us, His church. You, dealing with what happened with Lucas, is only a part of what you need to deal with. Lucas was my friend, Ry. I miss him a lot, but I've learned that talking about the good times and asking God for help has helped me heal. But you, you didn't mourn at all. You did the opposite. I tried to help but because of your guilt, you shut down. One minute, you were this vibrant, bold person and the next, this guarded, jaded shell of yourself. You just bottled it up and let it change you into a different person. It's been hard to watch you deal with his death. Trust me I know dealing with death is hard, but it's necessary to heal."

"Jay…"

"No Ry. Please let me finish."

I sighed…deeply. I really didn't want to hear this right now but, since I'm dealing with letting go, I need to. I also realized Jay needs this too.

"You have grown better but the mention of church in the past was met with that brick wall. You didn't just shut everyone out and pretend you were ok; you shut God out too. I don't even know if you realized it or not, but this is the first time you've been interested in knowing anything about church in almost 10 years. I was even more surprised you took this case because it was in a church. What changed Rya?"

"Well, I mean this church is where you all have been attending so there is that. I also think I understand why I started blacking out again and now having these dreams…"

"Are you serious? You think it has something to do with the case?" Jay asks with surprise and excitement.

"Actually, I thought it was Pastor Mark at first, but going to Bible Study with him the other day made me realize how much I care about the legacy I leave. I care about who I am in relation to how I live. I care about the fruit I bear. I mean, look at what's going on with Pastor Mark even though he turned his life around. I don't want to look back and regret my life. I believe that's what my dreams have been trying to show me. I see them more like events letting me know I'm headed in the right direction once they have happened, almost like I was meant to be in that place, at that time. It's like God is trying to tell me what to do to leave the right legacy or something."

"Kind of like visions?" Jay questions.

"Yeah… I guess so. Since the Bible Study, it made me question what my life will be full of. Will it be full of good fruit or bad fruit? God's fruit or the world's fruit? I never thought about my life in relation to the type of fruit I bear until recently. Maybe I need to reevaluate why, you know?" I respond contemplatively.

"Obviously! So, what's your game plan? This all sounds nice but what are you going to do about what you now know? Are you going to continue to pretend you're good, or are you ready to finally deal with this and come back to the Lord? Don't think these dreams were just visions of the choices you're going to make. These are the choices you should make. You're at a crossroads, Rya. I think the Lord is telling you it's time to choose."

Smiling at Jay, I hadn't realized how much he's grown through the years and how what he just told me was confirmation from the dream I had last night.

"When did you become so wise?"

Jay says with confidence. "You know, I think this case has made me wiser. I *feel* smarter. You'll learn a lot working with me."

We both laughed. He may not be my biological brother but he's the one the Lord has blessed me with and I'm grateful for that.

∞∞∞∞

It's a very special Saturday. Today is Jay's graduation and I couldn't be prouder of him. As I sat in my seat listening to the various speakers recite the speeches they prepared, I couldn't help but think about the preparations all these students took to get here. Everything they've done over the past 2 -4 years has been for this moment. The moment in which they walk across that stage to show everyone what they've done with their time. Their harvest is here; the fruit of their labor for everyone to see. I wonder how often I've faced consequences from these past years from the seeds I've sown when I turned my back on The Lord. How Pastor Mark is now dealing with his past. I want to sow good seeds but how do I do that? How do I prepare for something I'm so unsure of? What does it even mean to sow good seeds anyways?

The announcer says, "John Casey!"

Standing up and being absolutely ridiculous, I shout to the top of my lungs. "WOOHOO, GO JAY!"

Both my parents join in on my specialness in celebrating Jay as he walks across the stage. "ALRIGHT JC!!"

While watching the students walk across the stage to receive their diplomas. I have an epiphany. Lord, I want more than just a walk across the stage. I want an orchard of good fruit like the one You showed me in my dreams from the good sowing I've been doing. Please, show me how. I want more and I'm ready for real change in You, Lord.

After giving the final standing ovation for the graduating classes, everyone is leaving the stadium for their personal celebration plans. We take Jay to his favorite restaurant, La Dulce Vida, and make plans to do something together for the weekend. Today was a good day. We're having this wonderful time celebrating Jay and his accomplishments. It's usually in these mountain top moments when you realize at some point you have to come back down. You know something's going to happen when you ask yourself with a smile 'what could go wrong?' Of course, the sobering answer should be everything.

As we're getting ready to leave the graduation dinner with Jay, I get the update I've been waiting for from my associate at the DMV. The texts read:

'Hey Rya. That license plate number you gave me belongs to Patricia Sanderson. Sorry it took so long to get back. Lack of staff means I had an extensive list of paperwork to finish before I could run it. Her address was different from the one you gave me. I attached the address Patricia has this vehicle registered under.'

'Thanks Tom! It's no problem. Have a good one and don't work too hard.'

'Haha! You're funny. Tell JC I said congrats!'

'Will do.'

"Jay, we just got our break in the case. I'll tell you about it in the car. Are you ready to roll?! Mom, Dad, I'll meet up with you guys later!"

"I'm ready. Let's go!" Jay replies, indeed ready.

Finally, after this month-long process, we can get this case closed. Leaving the restaurant, we head back to the office to change and put all the information we have together so that we can call Beck and work out a game plan as to when we can go in and get Dante. Already changed and on our laptops, I let Jay in on what I found out.

"Alright, I just got word from Tom that the license plate is registered to Patricia. Now we can officially say we know Patricia is involved. We already knew Dante was the one driving because I saw him in the driver's seat. What did you get after cross-referencing Patricia's information with Dante's? The address provided on the DMV form is not her address. Let's find out whose address Patricia is using for her car registration."

Jay looking through his computer confirms what we already believed. "We know whose address that is, remember? That's Dante's listed address. If she's registering vehicles under Dante's address, they must be close. What does that tell us about her involvement at UFC and with Pastor Mark?" Jay says, looking concerned.

"I'm not sure but we can also conclude at this point that she knew we were suspicious of her. She was shocked to see me at Bible Study too. According to Pastor Mark, she hasn't been back to UFC since then, which was about two weeks ago. Given her history at the church, that's unusual behavior for her. Patricia also didn't show up last week for the youth event she was supposed to be helping with either. We should warn Pastor Mark just in case the family shows up again or worse; Patricia tries to convince Pastor Mark that she's not involved to get another chance to try to harm him."

We leave the office and make our way to Jay's car. It makes more sense for him to drive so I can make all the necessary calls on the way to Dante's address. While waiting for Pastor Mark to answer his phone, I got this ominous feeling.

Something bad was definitely about to happen. I just knew it.

Pastor Mark answers with that eerily calm voice again. "Hey Rya..."

"Pastor Mark, are you ok? What's going on? You don't sound like yourself."

"Patricia called me a minute ago. She told me everything. That Dante is the new Don and he's been trying to draw me out with those break-ins. Patricia joined the church with the intent to help Dante because I got her sister hooked on drugs when I was dealing. She also told me that if I give myself up, they'll stop the break-ins at the church. I know I should have called you, but I knew you would have tried to stop me."

"I was calling you to give you an update. We figured she was involved but who is she in relation to Dante? Why is she speaking for him? What else aren't you telling me, Mark?" I say feeling somewhat anxious.

"Patricia's his woman. She's been his woman all along. Rya, she's been at the church with the kids so she could find a way for him to get close to me. I'm putting my church family in danger. They came and shot up the church because of me! How can I live with myself knowing that? How can I preach to these people knowing I had a chance to do something to stop this and didn't? What if I don't go, and somebody gets killed by the family? I have to do something to make this right!"

"Mark, are you kidding me? If the family came to shoot up the church, do you really think they want to talk? You know the goal is to hurt you, to kill you, Mark. What happened to you doing the Lord's work, huh? What about all those kids who need you? You said nothing could stop you from doing what you were called to. Going over there is not a part of that. Let me and the police handle this! Mark, please don't do this!"

"I'm sorry Rya." Mark says, sounding dejected.

Listening to the sounds in his background, I knew he had already made up his mind. "Are you driving? Where are you headed?"

"She wants to meet at her house so I'm heading over there."

"We're on our way! Just don't do anything until we get there, ok?" I tell him while looking over at Jay. I give him a nod which lets him know we're headed for Patricia's house instead of Dante's since the call is on speakerphone. Thank God it's not far.

"Rya, no. Please don't come. I don't want you to get hurt. I can take care of this myself. I know I'm doing the right thing. I've made my peace with whatever happens." Mark says, trying to sound reassuring.

"Did you, Mark?! Where in the Bible is this one? Huh? I thought I told you to be wise. This is NOT using wisdom Mark! You said your purpose was to help these kids not end up like they would have! Who's going to show them how once you're gone or if something happens to you? Who's going to protect them then?! Think about this!"

After a few moments of hesitation, I thought Mark was going to stop or at least rethink his decision. After a moment passed where he wasn't talking, I heard Mark turn his car off. Remembering that this was his old neighborhood, he wouldn't have any trouble getting there.

"Rya... thank you for everything you did, but I can't let this go. I'm sorry. I'm at Patricia's house. I gotta go."

"Mark, NO!"

After Mark hangs up, I take a deep breath, so I don't panic. Thinking to myself I say, 'Lord if there was ever a time I needed Your help, it's now!' I turn to Jay who's looking pale because of how the conversation ended with Mark. Both of us appear to be trying not to lose the battle of allowing our concern and fear of losing Mark to get the better of us.

With backup called, and Jay's impeccable driving skills, we make a 30-minute drive in 23. Getting out of the car, we can hear loud voices coming from the backyard. Normally, I would wait for backup to get here, but I know Mark is back there by himself. Getting focused to pursue this altercation, I begin to pray:

'Lord, I need your strength to think rationally. Help me serve justice in a way that bears good fruit In Jesus name, Amen.'

With my prayer completed, I discreetly move behind car after car to get closer to where Patricia and Mark are standing outside. Conscious of Jay being behind me, I looked over my shoulder and tell him to fall back and keep a lookout for the police's arrival. As I get closer, I can hear Patricia's rage through her words. Looking back one more time over my shoulder, I see Jay has decided to find a hiding place behind some trees where he can be unseen to try and record the showdown on his phone. Not sure when the police will get here but we'll need the evidence.

"You RUINED MY SISTER'S LIFE!! She was NEVER the same after you got her hooked-on drugs." Patricia explosively yells at Mark.

Somewhat resigned and trying to make amends, Mark says.

"Look, I'm sorry if I got your sister hooked. I'm not that person anymore. That was a long time ago and I made some mistakes, but I don't remember who you're talking about?! I didn't even know you before you came to UFC."

Because she's upset and he doesn't know what she's talking about, she starts rambling and crying. I hope Jay is getting all this.

"She was a good kid. Started hanging with the wrong crowd and next thing you know; she's skipping school and coming home high. After a while she wouldn't even come home! Mom always sent *me* out to find her since I was the older sister. That's how

I met Dante. He helped me find her. She was in this rundown house high out of her mind because of you! Then I find out that you not only left the area, but you were trying to stop dealing so you could get *saved* and live 'for the Lord'! After everything you did! There was no way I was letting you just go off and live your life when you destroyed hers. So, *I* told Tony because he didn't know you were trying to leave the family and there was no way you were getting away with that!" Patricia expresses angrily.

At this point, I can see them, but they haven't noticed me. Kneeling behind a car on the other side of the street diagonal to Patricia's house, I try to work out a way to diffuse the situation before it gets any worse. Patricia's front door opens and Dante along with three of his men walk out the house. Oh no, this just got a whole lot worse.

Very calmly, Dante says, "That's enough Patricia."

Patricia turns around and puts her hands on her hip with an attitude to address Dante. "What do you mean that's enough? I had to put up with him at that church talking about how he's helping the youth. He wasn't helping the youth when he gave those drugs to my sister. He ruined her life and thought he could just go off and pretend like nothing happened! My sister didn't deserve that!"

Irritated, Dante says, "You don't even know what you're talking about. Now, shut up!

Furious and hurt for being told to shut up, Patricia replies, "What are you talking about? Why would you say something like that?"

"Lisa did what she wanted to. *She* brought her friends to get high. You're talking about her hanging with the wrong crowd; she *was* the wrong crowd. Hell, she was the ringleader! Even when she didn't have money, she found ways to get what she wanted. That brat got what she deserved."

One of Dante henchmen speaks up to say, "Yeah, she did *anything* to get her next high."

They all chuckle, including Dante. Patricia, however, looks at Dante with horrified surprise and pain.

"It was you? No, you told me Mark got her hooked. You told me to join that church so you could help me get my revenge. You told me to do whatever I needed to earn his trust. I did everything you asked me to, and it was you this whole time! You got her hooked! I did all this stuff for you! I almost shot him the other day for you! I should have shot you instead!!" Patricia raises her hand to hit Dante while all three of his henchmen pull out their weapons to defend their Don. Dante grabs her wrist, gets in her face, and says, "You put your hands on me, and you'll end up just like her. Now, I said shut up."

From what I can tell by Patricia's painful expression, his grip must be pretty tight. He looks at her with disgust and throws her arm so hard, she stumbles and almost loses her balance. Visibly trembling and crying softly, she looks at Mark and I can tell she regrets her decision to bring him here before putting her head down while holding her arm.

Dante, clearly over the moment, turns to address Mark. "You know Mark, I should thank you. Because of that bust almost ten years ago, I got arrested along with everyone else at the hideout. I guess beating someone to a pulp will do that. It was when I found out you were getting released that I got pissed. I mean, you were the reason we got arrested in the first place and you got off! And to *twist* the knife, 6 months after you left, we found out Tony went into hiding. That meant no money on the books or visits for the men that were loyal to him. Tony's hiding gave me the idea to create a bond with the men I was serving time with so when we did our time, they would be *my* family. When we all got out about five years later, I began carrying out my plan to take over. Because Tony was still in hiding, it wasn't hard to convert some of the family who got left behind. It didn't take long to figure out where Tony was hiding out either. Once I had his location, it was only a matter of staking it out to find out how many people I needed to take out to 'kill the king'. It was messy work, but we got the job done."

Dante's henchmen laugh at his attempt at a joke.

"So, you see Mark Knight, the only way I could lure you here and finish what we started 10 years ago was to attack what you loved. Patricia told me how you are with those kids. Scaring you didn't work so I knew threatening the kids would do it and here you are." Dante says while spreading his arms wide with pride like he knew it would work.

This dude is pure evil. At least all this talking gave the police a chance to get close because I can now hear the police sirens. This also means they can hear them as well. One of Dante's henchmen hands Dante a weapon. He has a few on his person so this one must be significant.

Looking down at it, Dante says to Mark, "This was Tony's gun. You know that special gun he liked to use thinking it would save his life. I figured it was only right if I finished the job he tried to do with his own weapon."

Dante begins to raise his arm to aim the gun at Mark's head for the kill. I look at Mark and run with everything I have. I can't let them kill him. I just…can't! I can hear his men yelling at me. I ignore everyone else and keep my focus on Mark. He's only one more step away. I have to make it. Right before the weapon goes off, I reach Mark and jump up to push him to the ground but not before I feel pressure in my left shoulder. Falling to the ground, Mark puts his arms around me to keep me from hitting the concrete. I hear Mark talking but I can't quite make out what he's saying. Before my eyes close, I hear:

"FREEZE! Put your weapons down, and your hands up!"

This time when I passed out is for a totally different reason.

9

Back To Square One, Huh?

Dreaming this time was pretty clear. I was walking down the aisle. Nope, not marriage: but covenant. I was officially giving my life back to Christ. We were at UFC. I had just solved the case and my family including Mark were there cheering for me. Or is it praising? Yeah, that sounds right: Praising God with me. I wonder since these blackouts started again with the start of this case, does that mean I won't have them anymore? This just seems like the end of the purpose of the blackouts for some reason. I guess we'll have to wait and see. Doesn't matter either way. They have been the blessing I never expected. They lead me back to Jesus.

Waking up right back where I started: this ugly all too revealing hospital gown! These things are the devil! Well, at least it makes sense this time. I kinda did get shot. There is one enormous difference though. Mark's here...and he's holding my hand. I guess he felt me move because I see that he lifts his head up to look at me. He looks like he's been here for a while too. His eyes are red like he hasn't slept. Is that the same outfit from when I got shot? Clearing my throat for double reasons, I tried to sound like I'm cool with him holding my hand, but my mind is going a little haywire.

"Ahem... Hey Mark."

"Hey Ry, I'm so glad you're awake. How do you feel?"

Still groggy but myself as usual, I say something uniquely me: "I feel like I got some really good sleep. What time is it?" I start looking around the room slowly for a clock. They usually have them in here.

"Uh, are you sure? You were shot and you're pretty nonchalant about it right now." Mark says to me confused.

"I'm good. The drugs are working so I don't feel it yet, just a little stiff. What are you doing here? I'm not complaining, but I figured you would be giving a statement or at home. Wait a minute, what happened with Patricia and Dante? Did they get away?"

Clearly seeing I'm a little distressed about the conclusion of what happened, he squeezes my hand. That squeeze was enough for me to forget about the outcome because I'm now distracted by our hand holding. Mark then informs me while I appear to be distracted that everything was taken care of and to just relax. Once he sees that I'm settled again, he slowly lets my hand go. For a moment, we just look at each other neither of us really knowing what to say. Right when Mark is about to say something, my parents walk in. Oh boy, it's about to get real now.

My mom comes in first, my dad right behind her. "Rya, you awake honey. Oh, Pastor Mark, I didn't know you were still here?" My mom says with a look on her face that says, 'what's going on here.

Realizing there were flowers on the table, I concluded that I didn't just take a nap. Now, I'm really wondering how long Mark has been here. Wait a minute, how long was I out? I still haven't found a clock.

"You've been out for 12 hours after you had surgery on your shoulder." My mom says pointing to my shoulder.

Eyes wide because I'm shocked, I've been out that long. I look at my mom while tilting my head to the side like, "How did you know that was what I was thinking?"

"You have that look on your face you used to give me as a kid when you wanted to ask me a question. I figured based off the circumstances that was your question. "Mom says, shrugging her shoulders.

Nodding my head ends that conversation but opens the door for another. I look away because I know the way my mom was looking when she first came in that it's going to come up. Instead of waiting for an invitation, my mom looks at the elephant in the room or should I say elephants and asks the question she's been wanting to ask since she saw Mark and I together.

"So, are we going to talk about why Pastor Mark is still here or are we going to pretend we didn't see anything? Simply curious." My mom says with her hand out like she's offering me the floor.

"Mark and I will talk about it. You can keep pretending that you didn't see anything." I say with a bright smile on my face.

Looking over at Mark, I say: "Thank you for waiting with me. We'll talk later if that's ok?"

"Yeah, that's fine. You rest up, ok? I need to call Pastor John anyway. He's been asking for an update. I'll be back later." Pastor Mark replies.

"Good. See you soon."

He squeezes my hand, bids my parents farewell and leaves. I watch him leave the entire time… What just happened here?

Mom starts off the questions of course: "Child, first off, how are you feeling?"

"Good. I'm just a little-"

Mom cuts me off before I even get to finish: "Secondly, what is going on with you and Pastor Mark?!"

Dad looks at me with the most serious face. "Yeah, is it serious? You can't have a fling with the Pastor now. That's not cool."

Why would my dad say something like that? What am I going to do with them? Clearly my mom wants an answer as she asks with her hands on her hips.

"Well?" My mom says…

"I'm not sure yet, ok? I mean, no flings dad, but I can't give you an answer until we talk. Will that work for you for now? Let us figure this out before I can respond. I just woke up, you know."

"It didn't look like it to me but ok. We'll leave you alone... for now. But next time we talk, I want ALL the details!" Mom says with a smile.

Thank God we have a good relationship because I seriously would think that's all she cared about. I know my mom. This is her way of dealing with me being injured. I look at her and hold out my hand. She takes it and squeezes just slightly.

"I'm ok mom."

With tears in her eyes, she rapidly nods her head as if she's reassuring herself.

My parents stayed with me for a few more hours. Mom decides I need to be pampered by doing my hair and dad wants to know the details of how the case went down before I went down. As they were leaving, my favorite doctor, Dr Chokmah, walks in to check on me since he knows I'm in the hospital.

"Rya, Rya. We couldn't find anything with the MRI we did a few weeks ago so you just go and get shot so we can find something, huh? You always keep me going, you know? Ever since you were a little girl, I knew you would keep us on our toes!"

Sounds like another parent, doesn't he? He acts like one too!

"Yes, I know," I laugh. "You tell me that all the time."

"Cause it's true. Now, how are you feeling?" He says with a serious expression.

"I'm doing ok. Just a little groggy."

Dr. C says, "Ok. Good. That's to be expected, especially after the anesthetics from surgery. Make sure you let your doctor know if it gets too unbearable. I can go get him before I leave if you want."

Smiling, I say, "I'm ok for now. Thanks doc."

While talking to Dr. C, My surgeon, Dr. Willis walks in. Saying hello to Dr. C, my surgeon walks up next to my bed with my chart. "Hello Rya. I'm glad to see you awake and talking. I'm pretty sure Dr. C asked but I wanted to check your pain levels, tell you about the surgery, and make sure you didn't need anything."

"Thank you. I'm ok. The morphine button is helping. I don't think I need anything but sleep right now." I speak.

Writing and nodding, Dr. Willis says, "That's good to hear. Now, I informed your parents, Jeff and Miriam about your report, but you were still asleep. The bullet that hit your shoulder missed your subclavian artery by a few centimeters. Had it been any closer, you would have bled out before I could've done the surgery to save your life. You were incredibly lucky, Rya Jones." He says with a smile.

I nod and smile, but I know luck was not the case.

"Excellent, we'll keep you here for at least a few more days before we can discharge you just to make sure there's no other complications with the surgery. We'll also do a CT scan to verify we didn't miss anything vital before you leave. Until then, relax and heal."

"Thanks Doctor Willis."

"Anytime Rya. I'm proud of you for what you did, you know. Even though you were shot, you caught the ones committing those crimes. It's all over the news! I hope you're proud of yourself too."

"I am. Thank you."

Dr. Willis leaves the room while Dr. C stays a little while longer.

"Most people like Dr. Willis will say you were lucky, but we know God's hand is on your life and He saved you, Rya. I hope you know that." Dr. Chokmah says with a fatherly smile.

"Yeah, I do. It's nice to have a reminder though."

As Dr. C is leaving my room, the nurse comes in to make sure I'm ok and not in need of anything. After giving them my food order, I finally have alone time. I ask God, 'was that good fruit?' I feel like it was. I mean I did the right thing for the right reason. I'm going to have to study the Word so I can understand what it means to bear good fruit.

While I'm in the mindset to learn and understand things, I have to address this Mark situation. I've been thinking about it since he walked out that door. Mark being here holding my hand and not leaving until he knew I was ok is… a lot. Though I appreciate him caring, is Mark really interested or is this some type of hero worship because I am no one to be worshipped. I did my job, plain and simple. But…what if it isn't? Am *I* really interested? Could something like this even work? I mean, I still feel like a heathen and Mark's a pastor. I fight crime and put myself in dangerous situations for others. Could he handle that? I didn't even consider the possibilities of dating or talking to anyone. I knew they were going to shoot; I just couldn't let Mark die…I have a lot of thinking to do. Before I can even get started sorting through my thoughts and emotions, Jay walks in.

"Jay, what's wrong? You look upset."

"Am I ok?! You are the one who was shot, Ry! Are you ok?? I thought I lost you! You were losing so much blood, and I couldn't help you. I could have done something Ry! I'm so sorry."

Oh goodness. What is going on here? Jay has always been soft hearted. He's easy to get along with and can handle himself in tough situations. I guess I didn't expect him to take it this hard. Clearly, I was wrong.

"Hey, come here. I'm ok."

He lays his head in my lap and sobs. I don't know if I can take any more emotional surprises. Jay never cries. Worry yes, sobs, uh… no. I did get shot in front of him though, so I guess he gets a pass.

"Jay, look at me."

He looks up with tears running down his face. Oh God, help me help him. With renewed strength I didn't have a moment ago, I cradle his face with my good arm and encourage him:

"Jay, the case with UFC was your first real assignment in the field. You just received your degree. I've been an investigator for the last ten years. This job has always been about sacrifice, courage, dedication, and perseverance. I've seen you do all those things more times than not with ease. Yes, getting shot was a traumatic experience and I hope we don't have another one any time soon, but it's part of the job and you are more than capable of handling it. We all freeze at some point. I did and I don't know anyone who hasn't, but you must work through your fear and allow God to grow you through it. It won't just go away. Be the brave young man I see every time I need something done in an unreasonable amount of time. You are more than a conqueror through Christ. Do you know that? Don't they teach you anything at that church?!"

He bellows out a good hearty laugh, and it warms my heart. He may not be my blood brother, but he's the one the Lord gave me, and I'll do anything to help him. Jay wipes his face and smiles at me, trying not to laugh again. I know he's still dealing with me getting shot, but he'll get through it. He always does. With the help of the Lord, of course.

"You did that on purpose! You know UFC's a good church especially since *your man* is one of the pastors. Just saying…"

"Oh my god! Did you talk to my parents? Did they tell you that?"

"Tell me what? I haven't talked to them yet."

Jay gives me his 'tell me' look. Why did I have to say something? I keep painting myself into these corners.

"My parents came in and Mark was here. They noticed he hadn't left yet and *demanded* to know what was going on. I told them they could pretend they hadn't seen anything and told Mark we could talk about it later. Why did you call him 'my man' then? Where did that come from?"

"I came in earlier to bring you flowers, and Pastor Mark was here holding your hand when I came in. He just looked at me, smiled, and turned his head back to look at you."

"Do you think this is hero worship? I mean I did kinda save him from getting shot. It's understandable."

"Uh, no. You don't remember my previous looks and comments about Pastor Mark earlier, do you?"

"What comments? I'm druggy right now. You'll have to refresh my memory."

Once he finished laughing at my drug comment, he lays it all on the table.

"First off, Pastor Mark gets hit on a lot and usually Pastor Mark just says he's not interested. With you, he made a conscious decision to compliment your looks first and then said he was saved so that's why he wasn't interested: not that Pastor Mark wasn't interested at all. I guess he assumed you weren't saved."

My mouth is wide open in astonishment because I surely didn't hear what Mark said in that way. All I know is I got dissed. So interesting how perspectives can change the way you should or could see something in another light. My mouth must have literally been open because Jay says to me,

"Close your mouth, I'm not done yet."

Yep, I just closed it.

"Secondly, he listens to you! You told him to go home, and he actually accepted your compromise and followed through. Pastor Mark practically lives at that church. Nobody can get him home by asking, except you."

"Not even Pastor John?!"

Shaking his head, no, Jay says, "Not even Pastor John. Pastor Mark just tells Pastor John that he'll leave for home in a minute-and that minute usually turns into hours. Pastor John just stopped trying. And another thing…"

Oh, my goodness, there's more…

Jay continues, "The day you told me you knelt with Pastor Mark at the altar when he was really upset, let me know a couple of things as well: One, Pastor Mark was vulnerable with you when he turned every other woman down. Two: you were vulnerable enough to initiate it. Rya, if Pastor Mark is falling for you, I can guarantee you're doing the same. Whether you realize it or not, you and Pastor Mark are really into each other. The question is will you trust the process and see where this relationship will go, or will you run and pretend like nothing's happening?"

I took a moment to think about what Jay was saying because I didn't see any of that. That's a lot to take in for someone like me. I'm a private investigator. I've seen what people do when they think no one is watching; so, getting too close to people is something I shied away from. Just looking back over this case tells me that people will do just about anything to get the results they want. Have I really let my guard down enough to allow Mark in? Oh Lord, I just realized I'm calling him Mark. When did that start? With my head in my hands, I address my elephant:

"Maybe you're right. Maybe I have allowed him in and not realized it. Maybe I have even opened up without trying. But Jay, I need to sort through whatever may be going on with me and Mark. This is uncharted territory and I'm just not sure I'm ready for a relationship yet, you know?"

Smiling like he understands, Jay replies. "I do and that's ok. You should talk to Pastor Mark about it though. "Don't avoid him," Jay says while giving me a dirty look.

What's up with all the looks these days?

"Ok, I won't avoid Mark. But I'm going to be in here for a bit and I'm going to take full advantage of it."

Jay laughs, kisses my cheek, and says he'll see me tomorrow. Yeah, can't wait for another pep talk.

10

All These Emotions

After a few days in the hospital, I awoke to see Pastor John walking in after one of my narc-induced naps. He looks like he's on a mission. Not sure how I feel about a personal visit from Pastor John but here goes nothing.

"Hi Pastor John, here to give me a report?"

"Yes and coming to check on you. I wanted to make sure you were doing well." He says with a warm smile.

"Thank you. I appreciate that. I'm doing well. Whatcha got for me?"

"Patricia, Dante and about ten other accomplices were arrested right after he shot you. Apparently when you ran to protect Mark and the family heard shouting outside, the rest of the gang came out of the house to protect their Don. Patricia being distraught about finding out her boyfriend was the reason for her sister's addiction, confessed to setting everything up. From getting Dante, her boyfriend, into the church; to trying to set Pastor Mark up by asking him out on dates so the family could take Mark out. When that did not work, Patricia asked to be Pastor Mark's secretary to learn his schedule and pick Mark off that way. The break-ins were designed to either scare Mark or make him angry enough to do something irrational: like come over to Patricia's house and solve the problem myself. Dante, as stated in the video Jay recorded, came after Mark because Dante was angry Mark got away with leaving the family for the past ten years. If Tony had not been in hiding before he was killed, he would have come after Mark a long time ago. He wanted Mark gone, plain and simple. As Dante revealed, her sister's addiction and eventual overdose was him all along. He just convinced Patricia that it was Mark because Dante needed another way to lure

Mark out of the church so he could finish what they started. Mark was already at the church by the time her sister was on drugs."

"That's good to know, Pastor. I'm just glad that justice was served. Is everybody ok? Is Mark ok? I know going through a traumatic experience can affect different people in a multitude of ways. Given the mass shooting with all the people there, I'm sure there are going to be plenty of people in need of help."

"I agree. I would like your help with that, but we will save that conversation for another day. I just spoke to Mark right before I came to see you and Mark let me know he was trying to finish a handful of things so he could get back up here to be with you." Pastor John says with a knowing smile.

"Ah, I knew this was coming."

Pastor John laughs. "Absolutely! Rya, did you know he held you until the ambulance came and went into the ambulance with you?"

"I had no idea. I had a conversation with Jay about it and honestly, I'm just not sure. I mean, I obviously care about Mark. I couldn't stand there and let him die. I just don't want his affections to be based on me saving his life, so he owes me type thing. I also don't want to base my feelings off of heightened circumstances, you know. I was truly doing my job."

"I understand that, of course. Rya, but let me share something with you. I am sure Mark wouldn't mind if I tell you:

Growing up, Mark's mom was the only one he had for years until I came along. Though I was there, it was still just Mark and his mom until Evelyn passed away not many years ago from cancer. Mark knew he would see his mother again, but he wasn't the same after that. Sure, he serves with a smile and gives his all; but Mark turned his focus to ministry and the children. No social life except when he comes over to have dinner with my family or Pastor meetings and fellowship - but that's it! I sometimes have to force him to do that! Mark and I are still close, but I know there's a part of him that is still too prideful to share certain things with me. You come to do a job for us and Mark's sharing things with you that took me years to learn! I've never seen him this open. Listen, I'm not saying to go and get married, but I am saying pray and search your heart. Ask yourself and the Lord if this could be more than a client/investigator relationship before you write it off. Can you do that for me?"

I didn't realize I was crying until he stopped talking and looked at me. I didn't know he lost his mom so recently either. Ok. I think I'm getting a better understanding of what everyone else is seeing. Closing my eyes and taking a deep breath, I look at Pastor John with a sincere heart and a smile and say to him:

"Yeah, I can do that."

After Pastor John left, I spent some time trying to sort through my thoughts and talk to Jesus. As I'm verbally processing what I'm feeling, I get the same out of body sensations I had the last time I passed out. Well, at least now I know what to expect.

I wake up in the dream where I'm sitting on a cloud. At least, that's what it looks like. Even though there is no one here, I don't feel alone at all. I feel at peace. Normally, with such empty space around me, I want to know what's going on. Being here, all I want to do is bask. Just sit and be at peace for once in my life. It didn't occur to me that I didn't have peace until now. Even though He's not here physically, at least not in a tangible sense; I know this peace is the Holy Spirit. It's like Him telling me what I can have if I come back to him wholeheartedly. And for the first time in forever, I genuinely want to. I'm ready to let go of the hurt, the anger, all the suppressed emotions I've held on to for so many years. All this time I've been trying to hide from The Lord and all He's been trying to do is give me peace. Give me Him. I get it now. I know I can't live the life I truly desire without Jesus, so I'm done trying to.

'Jesus, I believe you are the Son of God. I believe that you died and rose again for my sins. I ask that you come into my heart and make me new in You. I surrender my life to Your will for me. Have your way, In Jesus' name, Amen.'

∞∞∞∞

Coming out of that dream made me feel more rested than being in the hospital. It's been almost a week since I've been here but according to my doctor and nurses, I will get to go home soon. My parents, Jay, and even Pastor John came back to see me before I was discharged but no Mark. He called every day to check on me but spending his time at the church following this case has left him with a great deal of things on his plate. He apologized plenty of times, and I told him it was ok even though I was a little disappointed. In the end, I appreciated the separation. I think he may have needed it as much as I did. I'm pretty sure it gave Mark a lot of time to really think about us possibly being an item after spending all that time holding my hand while I was asleep. It gave me time to think and talk to my parents about what I was feeling. My mom, of course, had A LOT to say. She's been expecting us to get together for a while, apparently, and has been making plenty of comments since the case started about it. She told me Holy Spirit told her which is something she didn't tell me and clearly not my dad because he's been surprisingly quiet.

"Dad? What do you think about all this? How do you feel about me possibly talking to Mark?"

Dad gives me his serious face and says, "Sweetheart, I just want you to be happy. If anyone knows how hard the life of an investigator or any form of law enforcement is, it's me. It was challenging for Miriam and me because as law enforcement, I put myself in circumstances many people don't understand and can't handle. I just don't want you to give up who you are to please anyone. Don't get me wrong, I would love to see you get married. Not to mention, I want grandkids. Honestly,

I just want you to be sure because it's hard work baby, that's all."

"That's just it; I'm not sure about anything yet but I promised I would at least make an effort. Even considering a committed relationship is unfamiliar territory for me. I'm not sure what to expect. Will you help me?"

"You know I will always help you, but I won't lie to you. You may not like everything I have to say but know it's coming from a place of love, ok?"

"I know Dad. Thanks."

"Always baby girl."

I love being a daddy's girl.

∞∞∞∞

My surgeon finally let me go two days later and I've never been more ready to go home. Hearing the door open and looking up, thinking my parents would be walking in the room. I see Mark instead. Didn't expect that. While helping me in the chair to leave, I greet him with a question.

"Hi Mark! Wasn't expecting you to pick me up from the hospital. How did you convince my dad to let you do it?"

Laughing he says, "I got the third and fourth degree. Trust me, it wasn't easy for your dad to let his baby girl ride home injured regardless of if it was the Pastor or not. I think, in the end, your dad knew that I would still bring you home before curfew. Plus, I had your mom on my side."

Wheeling me to the front entrance of the hospital, he helps me in the car (one good arm remember) and straps me in. I give him my address to type into his GPS. This 25-minute ride to my house is going to be the longest and shortest drive ever. I'm a little nervous about this talk but interested in what he has to say. As we're driving toward my house, I realize I don't have to be 'Private Investigator' Rya right now. I can just be… me. This realization helps me relax and enjoy the moment. So, of course I had to tease. I couldn't help myself.

"Uh huh, and what is it you have planned sir. I mean, you cute but…"

He looks over shocked that I had the audacity to mention him dissing me by doing it to him.

"Oh my god! You gone bring that back up? I said I was sorry. I didn't know what else to say! Your comment caught me off guard and I was already wondering if I could get through this investigation without asking you out…"

At this point, I'm laughing because it's so heartfelt and I'm poking fun at him. He finally looks over, sees I'm laughing, and bumps my good arm with a smile.

"I'll never live that down, will I?"

"Nope."

Shaking his head in acknowledgement to my foolery, Mark comments: "Ok, I guess I'll have to make up for it then."

Ultimately, we get to the real conversation. I say:

"Ok, start talking? When, where, what, why, and how?"

Laughing he says, "To be honest, I've been having a hard time since the first day you walked into Pastor John's office for the job. At first, my defense was you were too young for the job even though I've seen you participate in other events for the youth in the community. If I'm being honest, I've noticed you for a while. But because we were all working, I could justify it and even resist the urge to talk to you or seek you out. You, being the investigator for our case, however, gave me no escape. For me, your presence was triggering because I had worked so hard to resist temptation in my walk with Christ. Finally meeting someone I was interested in, made me feel like I would be jeopardizing who I was in

Christ. I then had to deal with what was really bothering me about you being here. It was hard for me to separate my feelings versus what the Lord might be saying - especially for something like a relationship, you know?"

I can attest to that.

"Sure do."

"Anyway, then you come in for the job, clearly qualified, of age, professional, and a sense of humor. As the investigation went on, I also got to see different sides of your personality like how you're aggressively protective but can gauge a situation that needs a gentler approach. I was done for! I mean, what was I supposed to do with all that? You blew through every defense I set up without even knowing it. I found myself finding a reason to come and see you instead of just calling or texting you what I needed to say. On top of that, you had the nerve to call me out! You exposed me!" He laughs and so do I!

Then he continues: "My response was honest but defensive which was why I apologized. At the time, I wasn't sure if you were saved because I hadn't seen you with your parents at the church or at other church events, just the community ones. I figured my safest bet was thinking you weren't saved, so I settled on the fact that I was, even though I didn't ask if you were. The unsaved approach was all I had left to say when you asked if you were special because I came to the office after your blackout. I didn't want to say something crazy like, 'Yeah girl I came to see you!'"

Now, I'm laughing so hard my arm hurts! Waiting for me to pull it together for a serious moment, Mark continues:

"I know you're just as guarded as I am for other reasons, and I understand and respect that. I won't push you. I know we'll have a lot of work ahead of us. I'm actually talking to Pastor John about counseling for my issues about my past. I can't invite you into my life without first being able to deal with my own stuff, but I think if this is meant to be more, we can work through it with Jesus and the help of those we trust. What do you say? Care to give it a shot?"

Instead of just answering his questions right away, I felt it necessary to give him a better understanding of me: "It's a natural defense for me to shut most people out. Just recently, that included God. My relationship with the Lord has suffered for a long time because of my own doing and I'm ready to turn that around. With that in mind, I want to be friends first. My relationship with God must come first as I know you feel the same way about yours. I don't think we know enough about each other to sustain a healthy relationship, yet. Before we can even decide what 'this' is, I want any relationship we establish to be right in the Lord's eyes, not ours. I've already spent too much of my life thinking I knew what I was doing. Now, I'm starting to understand I can't do any of this without Christ. What do you think? Is that fair? Can you help me grow in my relationship with Christ, aside from having a relationship with me right away?"

We pulled into my driveway and Mark turns off the ignition. Turning to me, he smiles in agreement.

"I like that. Grow as friends first, build a good foundation, and go from there. I'll aim to make sure that our friendship always leads us back to Jesus. Just because I'm a Pastor doesn't mean I don't have plenty of growing to do myself and I want you to hold me accountable as well."

"I think I can manage that." I said as I returned his smile.

Putting his hand on mine, Mark gives me another serious look before he continues. "Rya, I just wanted to say thank you before we went into the house. You saved my life, and you didn't have to do that. I thought I knew what I was doing and that it was the right thing at the time. I just didn't want anyone to get hurt because of me. When I heard them shouting and turned to see you running towards me, I felt a level of fear I have never felt before. I was willing to lay down my life to right my wrongs but, in that moment, all I wanted to do was protect you. I would have done whatever I could've done to make sure you got out of there alive. When you pushed me to the ground, I knew in that moment that you mattered more to me than just the investigator solving a case. I just wanted to make it clear that what I feel for you has nothing to do with what happened the day of the family's arrest or you getting shot. What I'm trying to say is that us growing together is a confirmation of what I've known for a while. Our plan is to grow as friends first and I agree with that wholeheartedly. But Rya, I won't be backing down from my pursuit. I know who you are to me, and I intend to stick around until you know too."

For the first time in my life, I'm speechless. This is an answered prayer but hearing him say it is, wow. This will definitely be interesting… Mark's in pursuit. I'll have to remember that. He didn't wait for an answer to what he told me, just got out of the car, and walked me to my door. He walks me in first and makes sure I'm set before going back out to the car to grab my things. Bringing my hospital bag in, Mark says hello to my parents, gives me a very comforting hug, and tells me he will call me when he makes it home. Walking him to the door, I found myself unable to stop smiling. We say our goodbyes and I close the door watching him drive away through the peephole.

You know I'm not exactly sure how to feel right now. I've dated before but this feels different. From holding my hand as I slept, to getting me home safely. Even talking to my dad to get permission to bring me home from the hospital was an extremely sweet yet sobering gesture. Excitement for what may be and fright from the unknown, fight for dominance in my mind right now. If I'm being honest, I'm not sure who will win. I must admit, I enjoyed talking to and watching him as he took care of me.

Finally turning around to see my parents watching me as I walk over to the table is a welcomed and hilarious sight!

"I figured you'd be here if you weren't at the hospital." I laugh at my dad.

I laugh because I love my parents. They love hard but they don't play either. Clearly, my dad is not about all the fun and games. He's in protective mode.

"Of course! You thought Pastor Mark was just going to come, tell us he's good, and sweep you off your feet without us knowing or being involved?! Haha, yeah right!"

"No dad. I thought no such thing."

This is hilarious. The only reason they can get away with all this excessive parenting is because I'm injured. I don't mind the pampering or the home-cooked meals though.

"I made your favorite: grilled steak, garlic parmesan mashed potatoes and sautéed asparagus. The double crusted apple pie is in the oven. Come, sit down, eat, and tell us EVERYTHING!" My mom says.

Why is my mom so excited? She's cheesing like a kid locked in a candy store for 24 hours without supervision. Is she skipping to grab my plate off the counter? She appears to be ignoring my side eye glances too. I know mom's been waiting on Mark and me to 'find each other' but this is a little excessive.

Sitting down to eat, I fill them in on everything: From the conversation I had with Pastor John to the one with Mark in the car. I even tell my parents about the conversation I had with Jay. I then inform them that Mark and I agreed to be friends and naturally allow a relationship to grow into something else if that's where it leads.

"Girl, that's your husband. Y'all have work to do but so did me and your dad, honey. It'll work out." Mom smiles at me.

I just smile back and say, "We shall see mom."

Saturday is here and I'm starting to feel a little better. After being in the hospital for a gunshot wound to the shoulder, which could have taken my life; it's just good to reflect on the opportunity to come home. Given I still can't do everything for myself, my parents decided to stay in one of the guest rooms, just in case I needed help. Around lunchtime, Pastor John called to ask if he could come over to discuss a few things. He wanted to share a couple of updates with the congregation but wanted to inquire whether I would be interested first. Pastor John pulls up around 1pm and greets us all with warm hellos and hugs. He asks how I was feeling and if I'm recovering well. Of course, I tell Pastor John my parents are doing the best job because they are! Instead of lingering long, Pastor John gets down to the point:

"I had a meeting with the Pastors and Elders of the church. We've decided to call a church wide meeting to discuss what happened at the shootout, pray as a community, and encourage the members and others to clean up our streets. Turning this drive-by shooting and violence around and making it a community prayer meet is our main priority. The rebuilding of our community is not just a church-member response. I had been praying for a better way to draw in the community more. Though it was a distressing experience, I believe the drive-by and even the break-ins can be used for our good as a church and to the glory of Christ. This meeting will engage the community that no longer wants crime in their neighborhood and will help people to look to Jesus for that change."

"That's wonderful, Pastor!! I'm glad you were able to find a way to use the events of this case to get the community involved! That's going to be an awesome event."

"Yes, we give God all the glory for His providence. Actually, I wanted to ask you if you would be interested in being involved. I'm of course aware of your experience in law enforcement but I also know you have a Bachelors in Psychology because your mom told me. Putting all those things together, I genuinely believe your experience and expertise can be useful not just for this meeting but for UFC as a whole. What do you think?"

"Wow. I would love that, Pastor John! To be honest, I wanted to help; I just wasn't sure how. I'm not a Pastor or see myself having any other typical skills that I usually see in the church." I reply, stunned and flattered.

"Rya, you have more giftings than you know. God gave each of us gifts. Sometimes, we must be willing to pray and ask Holy Spirit to reveal those gifts to us. He didn't leave any of us without them. All gifts can be used in the body of Christ since we are of one body. As the Bible says, 'There are many parts but one body'. We don't need you to be a Pastor or a Greeter or a Deaconess unless that's where the Lord is calling you. We need you to counsel, to encourage others to believe in who the Lord created them to be, and to possibly even help those people learn to defend themselves if it comes to that. No violence per-say, but *'safe'* defense. Do you think you could do that?"

Trying not to bite my nails because I'm kind of anxious, I make sure I'm honest when I answer:

"Yeah, I think I could do that. I'm going to be honest here though: I'm nervous Pastor. I've never used these skills or gifts in this way before. Sure, I meet with clients to console or even encourage them to give me the information I need but that's my job. I just don't want to do something wrong."

"Rya dear, The Lord will lead you and we will all be there to help. You won't be doing any of this alone. We have staff at UFC that will train you to minister to people you have a hand in helping but allow you to flow as Holy Spirit gives you utterance."

I look over to my parents who are also sitting with us and they're both nodding their heads yes with a smile on their faces. My mom reaches out to squeeze my hand and I understand in that moment that The Lord will indeed give me what I need to do what He's calling me to do.

Looking back at Pastor John, I smile and say, "Ok, when do we start?"

11

I'm Ready

For the rest of the day, I spent a lot of time thinking about the events that occurred over this investigation. I usually do this anyway, but this time, I have nothing but time on my hands since I'm not quite in the clear yet. I keep a journal for my cases so I can always go back and reflect. The usual questions go like this:

'How did the investigation turn out? Was it solved or not? Was it satisfactory to your expectations? What did you learn from this investigation that you can take with you for future ones? In what ways can you improve your investigative skills that will help you for the next case?'

These questions are easy to answer: The investigation ended well - except for the bullet wound healing in my left shoulder. The case was solved and met my expectations because justice was served. The criminals are in jail and off the street. The victim, Pastor Mark, suffered no injuries. I learned to be more open minded and never let my limitations slow me down. I learned to recognize my weaknesses and work around them. I could have allowed these blackouts to not only slow me down but cripple me from doing my job. Instead, these blackouts led me back to Christ. I also learned not to ignore the questions nagging at me until I had an answer. Sometimes it's easier to just justify a person's behavior as just being natural. Being interviewed or interrogated can cause a person to act nervous or even look guilty. Interviewing Patricia left me unsettled. Some of the comments Patricia made and just her overall attitude told me to investigate why she would respond in the manner that she did. Those slight or abrupt responses can sometimes be the clues you need to follow that may lead to the evidence. If I had stopped looking into Patricia when I was first suspicious, we wouldn't have found some crucial information needed for solving the case. She led us to Dante; but the evidence also led us back to Patricia.

Getting started, this case with UFC felt like a normal job. Little did I know it was a setup through my fainting episodes to put me back on the right track with God. Too many times in my life I thought I didn't need Jesus. I had a rather good life, great relationships with family and friends, and a decent career. I mean, I'm a pretty good investigator. I could solve the world's problems one case at a time. I should be able to solve my own, right? I felt like I had everything I needed until someone mentioned Lucas. Mentioning Lucas or anything related to the accident left me hard hearted or completely broken. I would find myself reliving his death all over again as if it were yesterday. At least now I could talk about Lucas without having a complete meltdown. I know I'm not there yet, but now, for the first time in ten years, I could say that I'm on my way. And do you know what? It feels good too!

∞∞∞∞∞

Sunday's finally here and it felt like it took FOREVER to come! I'm now the excited one trying to go to church while my mom wants to watch UFC online because she doesn't want me to be in pain at church. Our compromise is to take OTC pain medicine to lessen the pain with my sling, so I won't fall asleep. Making our way to the car, I see Mark waiting outside. Oh boy, I'm not sure how to take this yet but I'll just be myself. No sense in changing that now.

"Hey Mark! What are you doing here? Came to make sure I made it to church? I mean I know I was a heathen for the last ten years, but I'm good now." I say with a smile.

I think I'm getting on my mom's nerves because her response reminds me of my childhood:

"Lord, have mercy. Rya, will you cut that out?"

Because I get my sense of humor from my dad, he thinks it's hilarious. "That was hilarious! Baby, you know she can't help herself. Remember when she was younger, and we would take her to church, and the Pastor would say something she didn't understand. Rya would ask us, with no filter, 'Dad, that didn't make sense. What does that mean?' Right there on the pew! Aw man, it was so embarrassing at the time, but she was serious when she said it! I don't think she can help her personality any more now than she could then! Haha!"

Pacifying my dad, mom pats his hand. "That's because she gets it from you, dear. What will I do with you two?"

"Love us!!" I say while making kissy faces at her, and she just rolls her eyes with a smile. I am so entertained right now.

"Is this how y'all are all the time because I can tell this will be a whole lot of fun going forward. I don't get to see this side of you, Mr. and Mrs. Jones. Seeing you at church is just Bible Studies and Sunday services. I don't go to the other events unless Pastor John makes me. I agree with you Sir; I don't think Rya can help it and I'm going to truly enjoy spending more time with y'all." Mark says with this amused look on his face.

So elated, mom gives Mark a hug. "Oh honey. That's so sweet. We will truly enjoy getting to know you better and spending time with you outside of church as well. Now, we love much but we chastise too. It's all in love. Just letting you know that moving forward."

"Yes ma'am."

Oh boy, this might be getting out of hand. Clearing my throat, I break up the happy moment so we can head to church. They can have more happy moments later.

"Uh, aren't we going to be late for church if we don't get a move on? We're starting heartfelt conversations in the driveway."

Dad puts his serious face on. Clearly, he doesn't want to be late.

"That we are. Let's go."

On our way to our vehicles, we all decide to ride together. My dad didn't want to let me go with Mark by myself again because, obviously, I'm a teenager for the second time. Trying to stay calm about going to church, my leg is moving in anxiousness. Looking out the window to avoid anyone, I realize how nervous I am. I almost feel like I should have prepared before going or something. I mean, I did pray and ask Jesus to come in my heart and I meant it. I don't know what's wrong with me right now. Mark must see what I thought were subtle leg moments because Mark touches my hand and says:

"Hey. It's ok, don't be nervous. You're here for the Lord, remember, not anyone else."

I turned to him. Maybe he'll understand. "How did you know that's what I was feeling?" I ask.

"It's the same way I felt when I walked into UFC for the first time when Pastor John was having Bible Study. Like I didn't belong there and that everybody else would think so too. Rya, church is for the broken, the sick, and the lost. Not the perfect."

I didn't realize I needed to hear that, but I did.

"Thanks Mark."

"Anytime."

Mom, obviously listening from the passenger seat, can't help but comment: "You guys are so cute!"

"Oh my gosh mom! We're driving ourselves next time."

My dad, however, is the one who responds this time: "We'll see."

We finally pull up to UFC and though the pep talk helped, the nerves still haven't left. I hope this is normal because it doesn't feel like it. Getting out of the car and walking into the sanctuary felt like a totally different experience. I guess because I wasn't here for work this time. I was here for me. For Christ.

Getting there five minutes before praise and worship begins, we spot Jay and wave him over. He joins our group while we all find seats that are next to each other. Mom, Dad, Jay, and Mark want to sit closer to the front since that's where they all usually sit. Me, I rather sit in the back unseen, but I follow the group with my head down hoping no one really sees me. I still feel out of place being here, even though I'm still excited about it. As praise and worship concludes and the congregation is told to be seated, Pastor John spots our group and moves to stand at the pulpit to address his flock.

"As we take our seats, I just want to welcome and acknowledge Rya Jones. Pastor Mark and I made the congregation aware of the investigation going on here and Rya not only solved the case with JC here, but she also stood in the gap for the church. We are forever grateful for Rya's service. Let's all stand and give her a round of applause please."

Oh no! I wish I could sink into the floor right now. If I had known he was going to single me out, I think I would have stayed home. Since that's not an option, I just smile, nod, and wave with my good arm while everyone in attendance takes their seats again.

"Rya will also be helping us with the community meet we have coming up so make sure you introduce yourself. She'll be more than happy to answer any questions you may have."

I look up at Pastor John like what are you doing? He looks at me with a smile and nod. If I had to guess what that means I would say he means to say, 'You can do this.' So, I nod back. He's right. I guess I can.

Pastor John spoke from Proverbs 3:5-6. He reminded us that if we lean on our own understanding, we will always be lost. To trust in The Lord's understanding is to know that His paths for you are perfect. The word was everything I needed to hear. I didn't realize how much I missed fellowshipping at church and getting a Word I can use for the week ahead. How fulfilling it is to be in the presence of God, worshiping with other believers. After all this time, I finally realize this is where I need to be, where I should have been all along. It's now the moment I've been waiting for. As soon as Pastor John goes to say, 'The doors of the church are open,' I'm on my feet. I make my way to the altar and the closer I get, the lighter I feel. The weight of my past feels like it's being lifted as I draw nearer.

Everything I've gone through with this case and my personal life has brought me back to my place with the Father. The investigation, watching Mark's fruit of his past unfold, talking with my parents and Jay has been steppingstones to where I stand right now. I can even go as far as to say seeing the conclusion of this case where two people literally wasted years focused on ending life instead of giving it. I spent the past ten years running from the Lord, but I don't want to run anymore.

It's time for a change. I'm here, Lord and I'm ready.

Now what?

Scripture References

1. Chapter 5~ John 15:5-8:

    *Bearing Fruit

2. Chapter 5~ Galatians 5:22-23:

    *Fruit of the Spirit

3. Chapter 10~ 1 Corinthians 12:

    *Spiritual gifts/Being of one body in Christ

4. Chapter 11~ Proverbs 3:5-6:

    *Don't lean on your own understanding

Made in the USA
Coppell, TX
31 May 2024

32968935R00132